Like no kiss I'd ever exp
introduction. It was a chance for my body to g
to his, for my senses to get the hang of his overwhelming
presence. His soft goatee brushing my skin when his jaw
moved, his tongue sliding past my lips. The faint suggestion
of cologne. Cool silk over hot skin beneath my hands

His hand drifted down my back. I thought he was
about to squeeze my ass, but he stopped at the small of
my back and pressed in with his fingers, pulling me to
him so I could feel his erection. I shivered. No, we were
not going to spend this evening discussing weather or
watercolors.

As gently as he'd started it, Sabian broke the kiss.

"If I was a cop," he whispered, "I wouldn't have
done that." He gave me a knowing grin. "And if you
were one, you wouldn't have let me, so I'd say we're in
the clear now, wouldn't you?"

"I guess that clears things up, yes." I couldn't
believe how badly my voice shook. Dropping my gaze
again, I added, "I'm sorry, this is so..."

"Don't apologize. A lot of clients are nervous the
first time." The softness of his voice matched his kiss,
and desire for the latter made my lips tingle. He raised
my chin so our eyes met when he said, "You gave
Becky your list of limits when you set this up. I won't
do anything you put on that list, and if there's
anything else you decide you don't want, all you have
to do is speak up. Okay?"

I nodded.

"So now that we've cleared that up," he said with
a playful lilt, "and we've established that neither of us
are cops, why don't you tell me what you *do* want me to
do?"

Loose Id ®

ISBN 13: 978-1-61118-397-9
DAMAGED GOODS
Copyright © April 2012 by Lauren Gallagher
Originally released in e-book format in June 2011

Cover Art by Anne Cain
Cover Layout and Design by April Martinez

DISCLAIMER: Many of the acts described in our BDSM/fetish titles can be dangerous. Please do not try any new sexual practice, whether it be fire, rope, or whip play, without the guidance of an experienced practitioner. Neither Loose Id nor its authors will be responsible for any loss, harm, injury or death resulting from use of the information contained in any of its titles.

This book is an original publication of Loose Id. Each individual story herein was previously published in e-book format only by Loose Id and is a work of fiction. Any similarity to actual persons, events or existing locations is entirely coincidental.

Printed in the U.S.A. by
Lightning Source, Inc.
1246 Heil Quaker Blvd
La Vergne TN 37086
www.lightningsource.com

DAMAGED GOODS

Lauren Gallagher

Chapter One

Eight fifteen, the blue numbers on the clock beside the bed announced without enthusiasm. Fifteen minutes till showtime.

It was a decent hotel. Not the Four Seasons, but not a roach-infested shit hole. A pair of queen-size beds. Thick drapes to block out the rest of the world and its prying eyes. A couple of watercolor prints so bland they almost disappeared into the pastel wallpaper.

It was the kind of place with people in nearby rooms and reassuringly thin walls. The murmur of room 412's television was just barely audible, and earlier, room 416's shower had added a whisper of white noise for a few minutes. At least this place wasn't Hotel No-One-Can-Hear-You-Scream, though if everything went according to plan tonight, the guests in the adjacent rooms would probably wish it was.

Rather than staring at the other bed, which was already turned down in undeniable anticipation of the next few hours, I focused on one of the watercolors on the wall, though I had virtually no interest in the lifeless image of some flowers in a vase. I'd once heard that there'd been studies performed that determined pastel colors had a soothing effect on people. Rumor had it some sports teams had painted the visiting team's locker rooms with that scheme in mind. I couldn't say if it ever worked on a rival football or baseball team, but it didn't do a damned thing to slow my pounding heart or unwind my knotted stomach.

What the hell am I doing here?

Groaning, but not loud enough for it to carry into neighboring rooms, I rubbed my eyes.

I had everything. The husband. The kids. The white picket fence and the moat of perfectly manicured grass encasing a flawless suburban four-bedroom on a street where nothing ever happened except gossip and barbecues. A sensible car. A refrigerator covered with grade-school pictures, grocery lists, and Garfield magnets. A calendar full of meetings with prestigious clients and blowhards.

Oh, and a drawer full of sexy lingerie I hadn't worn in years.

I *had* had everything.

I did still have most of it. The kids, the car, the house. The overloaded calendar and neglected lingerie. Thanks to that calendar, the grass wasn't so perfectly manicured anymore, but my son kept it trimmed enough to appease the homeowner's association.

The husband was long gone. Amicably divorced, happily remarried, completely oblivious to where I was tonight while the kids were with him.

Yeah, I had everything. Which was, of course, why I now reclined on a rented, rock-hard, queen-size bed, waiting for a male prostitute to show up.

No, not a prostitute. An "escort." So said the company's site, the woman I'd spoken to on the phone, and Kim, the friend who'd referred me to Elite Escorts to begin with. An "escort" who'd meet me in a hotel room and do anything I asked in exchange for three hundred prepaid dollars.

Not a prostitute at all.

Eight twenty-one. Nine minutes to go.

"Trust me, Jocelyn," Kim had said. "These guys are top quality. You won't regret it."

Wouldn't I? I wouldn't regret admitting I was so desperate for headache-free sex that I'd pay money to skip the crap and get to the fun part. I was buying sex. Nothing to be ashamed of or regret or hope to God no one ever found out about.

I groaned again, and this time the other guests might have heard me, but the TV noise didn't falter, nor did the silence in the other room. This was a bad idea. A really bad idea. What was I thinking?

I knew exactly what I was thinking. I was thinking about the fact that I hadn't had a decent night of no-strings, no-bullshit sex in entirely too long. I'd wondered for a while if it was even possible to have sex without first killing an evening feigning interest in the uninteresting, talking about anything except the reason we were both there, all the while dancing the dance of "I want this; do you want this?" until someone finally broke down and made a move. And even then there was no guarantee the sex would be good.

That was just the headache that went into trying to get a one-night stand. The very thought of what it took to kick-start a relationship these days made me want to scream.

Why was I here? Because I wanted to skip the song and dance, cut to the chase, and maybe have some sex that wasn't so hilariously bad it warranted a "you won't believe this" conversation with my girlfriends. I had more of those stories than I cared to admit.

Eight twenty-four.

I checked my cell's sent messages for the thirtieth time to make sure I'd sent the right room number to the phone number the agency had given me. The room was correct, the message had transmitted, and my stomach tightened a little more.

Now that he was mere minutes away, another thought occurred to me: what if I wasn't attracted to this guy at all? Every photo on the site had been gorgeous, but that didn't mean a thing. I'd done enough online dating to know how deceptive a profile picture could be. It wasn't that I was excessively picky, but the fact was love was blind, lust was *not*. I didn't need Adonis, but I could do without the Elephant Man.

Kim had spoken highly of the agency, though, and she was the princess of pickiness. Any man for her had better be well-dressed, well-groomed, and well-hung, and if he couldn't get her off at least twice with his mouth, she wouldn't return his calls. Couldn't imagine why she was thirty-nine and still single.

That pickiness was why she'd started using Elite Escorts to begin with.

"Once in a while," she'd told me, "I just want a long night with a beautiful man who wants nothing more than to make me come and fuck me senseless." And in spite of the fact that I eventually wanted a husband, or even a lover who stuck around for more than a few months, that was all I wanted tonight.

Of course, that wasn't addressed directly in my interactions with the agency. We'd discussed the things I didn't want and didn't allow, all the while very carefully avoiding saying I wanted to have sex with the escort or that he'd be willing to do so. I paid for his company tonight. What happened during the allotted time was up to me, and it cost the same if we spent the evening playing chess, discussing the weather, or...not.

All the cloak-and-dagger of coded phrases and carefully worded questions added to the thrill, but it also made me nervous. What if I got caught? What if my man of choice tonight—a tattooed, goateed escort named Sabian—had a badge in his pocket instead of condoms?

An arrest for soliciting sex from an undercover cop. Oh, Lord, I could only imagine how that would go over at the advertising firm where I worked.

Fuck, what am I doing? I had kids to think of. And a career. My ex-husband had never tried to take the kids from me, but if he found out about this little indiscretion, then what?

I glanced at the clock. Eight twenty-seven. Blood pounded in my ears. Sabian would be here any minute.

I could always go the cowardly route and simply take what I'd paid for: his time and company. Sex wasn't required. It wasn't all that unusual for an escort to do exactly as his name suggested and escort his client to a restaurant, the opera, wherever. Perfectly legal. Perfectly socially acceptable.

And perfectly boring.

Eight twenty-eight.

Any second.

To hell with chickening out. I hadn't shelled out this much money to sit with the guy and talk about bland watercolor flowers. Odds were, he was legitimate, and my libido was pretty persuasive with its suggestions that it was worth the risk that he wasn't.

Eight twenty-nine.

But if my ex found out. If my boss found out. If my kids found out.

Eight thirty.

I need this. I want this. I'm going to do this. Shit. I can't do this.

A sharp knock startled me.

Too late for second thoughts.

Gulping back my nervousness and ignoring the swarm of cracked-out butterflies in my stomach, I rose and approached the door warily.

I took a deep breath. Turned the deadbolt. Opened the door.

Madre de Dios.

Standing across the threshold was the kind of man who'd never have noticed me if I hadn't just put a few Benjamins into his pocket. In photos, he was gorgeous. In the flesh, absolutely stunning. His light brown hair was playfully mussed, the look that was just shy of an engraved invitation to run my fingers through it. His hazel eyes edged closer to green now than they had in his photos, which was probably just a trick of the light. He was several inches taller than me with a flat stomach and broad shoulders, and I immediately had the impression he could throw me around and get rough if I wanted him to, and I did. Hell yes, I did.

The Elephant Man he was not.

Most of the guys on the site were completely clean-shaven, but Sabian had a neatly trimmed goatee. It was thinner than it had been in his photos, like he'd recently shaved it and was letting it grow back, and it framed the most mouthwatering set of lips I'd ever seen on a man.

"Some clients don't like the escorts to kiss them," the woman at the agency had said. "Is that something that would be an issue?"

"No," I'd said, "kissing is fine."

Looking at his mouth now, wondering just what those lips were capable of, kissing was more than fine.

He raised an eyebrow. "Deanna, I assume?" Disappointment fluttered in my stomach for a split second, thinking he'd come to the wrong room, before my brain caught up and reminded me of the false name I'd given the agency.

"Deanna. Yes."

"Sabian." He extended his hand, and light skittered up the deep blue fabric of his shirt. Silk, I guessed, from the way it caught the light. The material begged me to touch it, to run my hands over it, and I wondered if that was why he'd worn it. This whole situation got a hell of a lot weirder when it dawned on me that I *could* run my hands over it, could touch it and anything under it as much as I damn well pleased, because I'd paid for the right to do so.

I just shook his hand before gesturing for him to follow me into the room. He closed the door with a quiet *click*, and my heartbeat drowned out the television in the next room.

Neither of us spoke. I stopped and faced him, unsure just where we went from here. This was one part I hadn't considered: getting from the initial introduction to the reason I'd paid him to be here. The whole point was skipping all the games and headache that inevitably accompanied even a one-night stand, but presumably we didn't just drop trou and go at it. Or maybe we did. How much of an overture did something like this require? Was there some kind of sacred prostitute-client etiquette I didn't know about?

I bit my lip and folded my arms across my chest, fidgeting between the man and the bed. "I, um..."

He smiled. "You've never done this before, have you?"

My face burned. "Not with..." I gulped. "A professional."

"There's a first time for everything." He took a tentative step toward me, pausing to let me breathe before he took another. "Just tell me what you want."

I searched his eyes for signs he was searching mine. Was this the part where I incriminated myself and said I wanted sex, at which point the cops came in and busted me? Or he handcuffed me in a decidedly unsexy manner?

Finally I said, "I want what I paid for."

He laughed softly. "You're already getting what you paid for." He gestured at himself. "I'm here for two hours or until you kick me out, whichever comes first."

I moistened my lips. "Well, I wasn't thinking of kicking you out. I can't say I'm sure how we...where we..." I paused, clearing my throat. "I'll be honest, I'm completely clueless about this." There was something oddly liberating in admitting that. It was a reminder he wasn't here to judge me, that his opinion or evaluation of me was irrelevant. I didn't have to impress him.

Which was good. I didn't doubt my sexual prowess, but I doubted there was much I could do in bed to impress Sabian of Elite Escorts.

He shifted his weight. His eyes darted over my shoulder, presumably at the downturned bed. When he looked at me again, he raised an eyebrow and gave me a playful grin. "Are you worried I'm a cop?"

My cheeks got hotter, and when I dropped my gaze, I nodded. "A little, yeah."

Without speaking, he put a hand on my waist, and I think I inhaled all the air in the room in one sharp gasp. When I'd relaxed—sort of—he did the same with his other hand. I couldn't say if he pulled me to him or if he came to me, or if the space between us simply folded in on itself until it ceased to exist, but somehow we were against each other, and he kissed me.

His kiss was gentler than I expected. That may have been because I had no idea what to expect anyway, but I definitely hadn't bargained for the soft, still presence of his lips against mine. I tensed as soon as our mouths made contact, and he waited for some of that tension to ease before he made another move. After I'd tensed and relaxed again, he deepened the kiss, and I almost fooled myself into believing I wrapped my arms around him just to keep my balance.

Like no kiss I'd ever experienced, his was an introduction. It was a chance for my body to get accustomed to his, for my senses to get the hang of his overwhelming presence. His soft goatee brushing my skin when his jaw moved, his tongue sliding past my lips. The faint suggestion of cologne. Cool silk over hot skin beneath my hands

His hand drifted down my back. I thought he was about to squeeze my ass, but he stopped at the small of my back and pressed in with his fingers, pulling me to him so I could feel his erection. I shivered. No, we were *not* going to spend this evening discussing weather or watercolors.

As gently as he'd started it, Sabian broke the kiss.

"If I was a cop," he whispered, "I wouldn't have done that." He gave me a knowing grin. "And if you were one, you wouldn't have let me, so I'd say we're in the clear now, wouldn't you?"

"I guess that clears things up, yes." I couldn't believe how badly my voice shook. Dropping my gaze again, I added, "I'm sorry, this is so…"

"Don't apologize. A lot of clients are nervous the first time." The softness of his voice matched his kiss, and desire for the latter made my lips tingle. He raised my chin so our eyes met when he said, "You gave Becky your list of limits when you set this up. I won't do anything you put on that list, and if there's anything else you decide you don't want, all you have to do is speak up. Okay?"

I nodded.

"So now that we've cleared that up," he said with a playful lilt, "and we've established that neither of us are cops, why don't you tell me what you *do* want me to do?"

I'd never been the one to take the reins in the bedroom. Ever. The faint scent of his cologne made me want to tear that blue silk shirt right off him and demand he fuck me, but nerves conspired to keep me still and tongue-tied. I must have looked like a complete idiot to him.

If I did, he didn't let on. Instead, he kissed me again, and at least one of us wasn't tongue-tied. When his hand moved on my back, I half-expected the "is this okay?" touch beneath the back of my shirt, but it moved up instead of down. Right up the center, leaving a trail of goose bumps along my spine and across my ribs before trailing over the back of my neck and into my hair. Barely there fingertips brushed over my scalp, making my breath catch and sending a shiver right through me.

Then his light touch became a firm grasp, and in the same instant that he pulled my head back, he broke the kiss and descended on my neck. I whimpered and dug my fingers into his shoulders, certain every bone in my body was a heartbeat away from liquefying.

Oh, Lord, the things this man could do with his mouth. He searched my neck for erogenous zones, and whenever he found one, he teased it with the tip of his tongue, his lips, even his goatee. His shirt bunched in my hands as I tried to keep myself upright. It seemed a shame to wrinkle such fine fabric, but it was about to be in a rumpled heap on the floor anyway, so to hell with it.

I grabbed the front of the shirt I'd already started wrinkling and took a step back, hauling him with me. That first step was a leap of faith, and once it was taken, I was sure I could do this. I could *definitely* do this. The second was more confident. The third was shaky because his lips were on my neck and his breath was on my skin and his hand was on my hip, sliding around to my lower back and keeping me against him, close to him, as close as two fully dressed people could be.

He raised his head and reached into his back pocket. Then he leaned past me to set a few condoms on the table between the beds. Their presence made this all more real. I was suddenly less certain I could do this and doubly sure I wanted to. Especially when I glanced at them again and recognized both the logo and distinctive gold foil. I'd only been with a few men who'd needed Trojan Magnums and one who *thought* he did. With Sabian's hard cock pressed against my hip, there was no mistaking that his condom preference was more than just an ego extension.

With uncertain fingers, I went for his top button. The first few buttons were easy. The more they fell away, revealing more and more of his chest, the more both my knees and hands shook. They didn't get any steadier when he gently freed my blouse from my skirt. The warmth of his fingertips on the small of my back straightened my spine, and when he slid his hands up my sides, lifting my blouse up and off, I suppressed a whimper.

Shoes came off. His belt and pants. My skirt that was ridiculously long for this situation. Without that skirt, I still felt ridiculous, this time because of my simple white cotton bra and briefs. I'd thought about wearing something out of the sexy drawer but chickened out at the last minute.

Sabian didn't mind. He unclasped my bra with ease, dropped it on top of the rest of our clothes, then pushed my strictly utilitarian briefs over my hips.

The man obviously had a thing for silk, and I couldn't resist running my hand over his hip, telling myself I just wanted to feel the smooth, warm texture of his black boxers. Sabian wasn't so easily convinced, though. He must have known what I really wanted, because he closed his fingers around my wrist and guided my hand to the front of his shorts. The first thing that crossed my mind when I squeezed his erection through his boxers was, "this is going to hurt." The second was, "I can't fucking wait."

I closed my eyes, forcing a deep breath into my lungs. This was a dream. Men like this simply didn't exist. They sure as hell didn't join me in a hotel room with a mouthwatering hard-on in silk boxers.

"Doing okay?" His voice startled me. My eyes flew open and met his. His eyebrows lifted with concern and alarm.

"I'm fine. I'm fine." My cheeks were on fire. "Just...still...this is..."

"It's new. It's okay." Like his words, his smile was anything but patronizing. "You're allowed to be nervous."

I laughed softly. "Thanks."

He drew me closer, kissing me again. Warm-cool silk brushed my bare skin, making my breath catch. Without breaking the kiss, I slipped my fingers under his waistband. I wasn't sure if it was boldness that drove me or just the need to not be the more exposed person in the room, but the end result was the same.

When he stepped out of the black silk pooled at his feet, and I stepped out of the white cotton around mine, he guided me to the side, keeping an arm behind me as he used his body weight to ease me down to the bed. Together, we sank onto the mattress. The sheets were cool against my skin, emphasizing the heat of his body over mine.

He overwhelmed me, and I was thankful he kept right on kissing me. Some clients may not have liked kissing their escorts. I loved kissing anyway, and with as nervous as I was now, at least it kept my mouth busy and kept me from saying anything stupid or awkward.

He broke the kiss just enough to speak. "You're calling the shots," he murmured against my lips. "Just tell me what to do, and I will. We can do this as fast or as slow as you're comfortable. Anything you want."

"I'm not..." I took a breath. "I'm not very good at, um, at asking for what I want."

He raised his head. "Then why don't I do what I think you'll like, and if you don't, you can redirect me?"

Sabian, you're worth your weight in gold. I just nodded.

He kissed me gently, then worked his way to my neck. He rested his weight on his forearms and, one gentle kiss at a time, moved down my neck, over my collarbone, to my chest.

He ran the tip of his tongue around my nipple, then blew on it, and the cool air on moist skin made my breath catch. I combed my fingers through his hair as he pulled my nipple between his lips and teased it with his tongue, and I had to bite back a helpless moan when his talented mouth sent shivers down my spine. My toes curled, my back tried to arch beneath us, and I had to know what else his mouth could do. Now, Jesus Christ, now, I needed to feel those lips and that tongue on my clit.

But Sabian was in absolutely no hurry. Even after he'd finished teasing each nipple in turn, he took his time, letting me savor every soft kiss on the way down my chest and belly. It was heavenly, sending little shivers and lightning bolts all the way to my feet, but I wanted his tongue on my clit. I desperately wanted him to go down on me, and hell if I could figure out how to say it, so I had no choice but to surrender to his slow downward migration of light kisses.

By the time his lips touched my inner thigh, my entire body quivered with anticipation. When his tongue met my pussy, my back arched. He put an arm over my hips, holding them steady while his tongue's gentle explorations made me squirm. He hadn't even touched my clit yet, and I was already losing it. With every passing second, I fell apart a little more, wondering if he'd ever stop teasing me and just—

"Oh, my *God*..." The arm across my hips was all that kept me from flying up off the bed when his tongue fluttered across my clit. If his kiss had made my knees shake, the gentle, sweeping circles he made with his tongue shook me right to the core. Two fingers slipped inside me, and a soft half moan vibrated against my clit, and my entire body trembled in response to his voice and his touch.

A helpless sound escaped my lips, and I clawed the sheets. I didn't think it was possible to be this aroused, and in no time at all, he effortlessly brought me to a shuddering climax. I couldn't have held back if I tried, nor could I have stopped the throaty, passionate cry that was probably heard for miles around.

Even when I came back down, while my eyes tried to focus through the blur of tears and my fingers released their grasp on the bed, Sabian didn't stop. His tongue made gentle circles, backing off just enough to keep me from getting too sensitive, and his fingers continued teasing my G-spot.

"Sabian, I—" I stopped, biting my lip. *What? Keep doing that? Stop and fuck me? Don't stop? It's too much? It's not enough?* The only thing I knew was that my need to have him inside me became more urgent with every touch of his tongue. I needed him like I needed the air I couldn't quite remember how to breathe.

Finally, I managed to choke out two words: "Fuck me."

He didn't stop immediately, but the slower, gentler strokes told me he'd understood and was obeying. His fingers withdrew, and his tongue eased off my clit one circle at a time, letting me return to earth without an abrupt, jarring halt.

He pushed himself up on his arms and came back up to me. He might have intended to kiss me, or maybe speak, or, hell, I didn't know what. I didn't give him a chance.

Grabbing the back of his neck, I dragged him down into a deep kiss. He didn't even flinch. His tongue slipped past my lips, and the sweetness of my pussy drove me wild, reminding me of the still-tingling remnants of my orgasm.

We were both breathless when he broke the kiss and looked down at me. "How do you like it?" He trailed a finger down the side of my neck. "Rough? Gentle?"

I licked my lips. "Rough."

He grinned. "Rough I can do." He reached for the bedside table.

It occurred to me while he went through the foil-tearing condom-rolling motions that this man who was about to fuck me was a total stranger. We didn't know each other's e-mail addresses or wine preferences. We didn't know all the boring things we might have feigned interest in over dinner and drinks on a normal date. We didn't even know each other's real names. The only things I knew about him were what he did for a living, how gorgeous he was naked, and the fact that he was about to fuck me.

And I couldn't have been happier.

With the condom in place, he got on top again, but he didn't fuck me yet. His lips closed around my nipple. He held it with his teeth and teased with his tongue, finding that perfect balance between pain and pleasure, and though I wanted his cock *right now*, I loved what he was doing too much to ask him to stop.

He must have spent a good minute or two there before he moved to my other nipple, and all the while, my pussy tingled with anticipation, knowing he could be inside me at any second. The condom was on. I was wet and turned on. Any. Fucking. Second.

But he hadn't been in a hurry all evening, and he didn't start now. Even when his lips left my nipple and started up toward my neck, he took his time, letting each soft kiss raise its own goose bumps before inching higher, higher, still higher. Electricity crackled along my spine and under my skin.

Sabian, if you kiss my neck right now, I swear I will...

Oh.

Oh.

Oh...God...

His lips on my skin. Collarbone to my ear. Back down. Other side. Soft goatee, hint of stubble, warm lips, oh...God...

There must have been some mantra repeating in his head, something like *think about what she wants, think about what she wants, think about what she wants.* Maybe there was. This was, after all, his profession.

Now if I could just find this without having to pay for it...

That train of thought was abruptly derailed when he pressed his cock against me. A momentary flutter of panic—*Am I really about to have sex with a complete stranger, and a prostitute at that?*—went through my mind, but it only took the head of his cock sliding into my pussy to erase any thoughts of...well, anything.

As he'd done with everything since he'd walked through the door, he took his sweet, sweet time. Withdrawing, moving a little deeper, withdrawing again. It was an absolute age before he was all the way inside me, and by the time he was, my head spun, and every breath I pulled in was made of his cologne.

He bent to kiss me. As his tongue parted my lips, he withdrew slowly, and I grabbed on to his shoulders just to anchor myself in the here and now. Christ, I didn't know if I was just that turned on, or if he really felt that good, or if he was really that good of a kisser, or—

He thrust into me so hard the darkness behind my eyelids turned white for a split second, and he didn't give me time to recover. I moaned beneath him, digging my fingers into his biceps and holding on for dear life while he fucked me like I had *never* in my life been fucked. The headboard banged against the wall. The bedframe creaked and groaned. I probably cried out, probably whimpered.

Through clenched teeth, he said, "Tell me if I'm doing it too hard."

"No, no, this is perfect." Dear God, was it ever. No one had ever hit every spot inside me like that. Any guy who was big enough to fuck me so hard it hurt usually didn't bother getting me wet enough first. Sabian, though, holy hell. He'd made sure I was more than wet enough to accommodate him.

He was perfect like this, but I wondered if a different position wouldn't make this even hotter.

"I want you to—" I paused.

Sabian slowed down, lifting his eyebrows inquisitively and bidding me to continue.

I licked my lips. Asking for what I wanted in bed was unusual. Demanding it was downright alien. This was bought, paid for, and on my terms, though, so I took a breath. "I want you to get behind me."

He nodded, and when he pulled out, I whimpered. He'd be inside me again in a second. Just had to change positions. I pushed myself up and turned around, ignoring the precarious shaking in both arms and legs.

Sabian didn't waste any time. His hand had barely made contact with my hip before his cock—oh, God, his thick, perfect cock—was deep inside me again.

He started out slower this time. With the heel of his hand, he put gentle pressure between my shoulder blades, encouraging me to lower myself from my hands to my forearms. Thankfully he couldn't see my face at that point. I must have been beet red, cringing inwardly at the embarrassment of being like this with my butt up in the air.

All it took was one deep, hard thrust at that angle, and I didn't give a damn how ridiculous I looked. I know I cried out that time. My pussy could barely accommodate him anyway, and in this position, he hit every perfect place like my body had been designed with his cock in mind.

"Like that?" he asked, panting as he kept right on fucking me.

I tried to speak. Managed a nod. Then I forced myself to remember how to inhale just enough air to get three words out: "Pull my hair."

His rhythm didn't falter for a second when one hand left my hip and went into my hair, twisting it around his hand and making my scalp tingle. Tears blurred my vision. My fingers clawed at the sheets and pillow, finally hooking over the edge of the mattress so I could find some leverage and rock back against him.

"Harder," I moaned. "Harder, please..." I didn't know if I meant for him to pull my hair harder or fuck me harder, but he did both.

I was so close—so damned close, so frustratingly, painfully close. I couldn't come from this alone, and I was always too embarrassed to touch myself in front of someone, but—

Oh, fuck it. What did I care? Wasn't like we'd ever see each other again.

I shifted my weight onto one arm and reached for my clit with my free hand. In seconds, the first deep tremor rippled through me, and I couldn't even draw a breath before another tremor, then another knocked the air right out of my lungs. I couldn't breathe, couldn't think, knew nothing but the heart-stopping sensation of Sabian driving his cock into me.

Then, when I didn't think it could possibly get any more intense, some unseen dam broke inside me, and as my lips parted in a soundless cry, I came.

I was usually a moaner, a screamer—the kind of lover whose worst fear was thin apartment walls, but Sabian rendered me completely silent. The only sounds were his sharp, rapid breaths and the banging of the headboard and the beating of my own heart. I was simply too overwhelmed to muster anything more than a sigh and too intoxicated to care. It was only when the world stopped spinning and I could see through the tears in my eyes that I finally whispered, "Oh my God."

When I opened my eyes, the sheets were bunched in my trembling hands. I couldn't remember when my fingers had left my clit to grab the edge of the bed, but there they were. Hell, I could barely remember how to breathe. And he didn't stop.

He just. Didn't. Stop. Right through my orgasm, long after I was sure I'd collapse from the inside out, he kept fucking me. I couldn't tell my own heartbeat from the headboard hitting the wall, couldn't tell where his panting ended and mine began.

For the first time, his rhythm faltered. He slowed down, and over my own heavy, irregular breathing, I heard his breath catch. His hands tightened on my hips. Then he drew and released a deep breath, picked up speed again, and my vision once again clouded over.

Until he faltered again. Recovered. Slowed down.

A heartbeat's worth of clarity pierced my fog of ecstasy long enough to make me realize he was close, *that* close, but probably held back until I gave him the word. How he'd made it this far, when any guy I'd ever been with before would have long ago been snoring away beside me in post-orgasmic bliss, I had no idea.

I licked my dry lips and somehow managed to speak.

"I want... I-I want you to come."

He didn't hold back. At all. He fucked me harder than before, faster than before, and it was enough to bring tears to my eyes. His fingers dug into my hips, his breath caught, and with a low groan that reverberated through every nerve ending in my body, he took one last thrust and came.

Everything was still. The room was completely silent except for my thundering heart and Sabian's sharp, uneven breaths.

Steadying me with a hand on my hip, he pulled out.

"Get on your back again," he said. "I'll be right back." While I changed position, he got up to get rid of the condom.

I glanced at the clock I'd warily watched before his arrival. Still plenty of time between now and when the proverbial meter ran out. So did we both catch our breath? Talk about the watercolor on the wall? Another area where my knowledge of prostitute-client protocols was sketchy.

Sabian, of course, didn't have any such issues. He rejoined me in bed and kissed me deeply as he put an arm over me.

"Doing okay?" he asked.

I nodded. With a shy laugh, I said, "Definitely getting my money's worth."

He chuckled. "That's what I like to hear." He craned his neck to look at the clock. "And it looks like you have plenty of time left, so..." He kissed me again.

Where he got his energy, I had no idea, but he didn't quit until the time was up. By then, God knew how many orgasms I'd had, and Sabian had come twice. I couldn't help noticing he was hard again when he got up to get dressed. A shiver ran down my already tingling spine. How much longer could he have gone? Did I dare cough up the money and find out?

Tempting though it was, another round with him probably would have killed me. As it was, I had no doubt I'd be sore tomorrow, and it was worth every minute. Every minute and every dollar.

Watching him button his silk shirt, I grinned to myself. *That was two hours and three hundred bucks* well *spent.*

With his time up, Sabian made a quick but polite escape, leaving me with his kiss still lingering on my tongue in the room with boring watercolors and haphazard sheets.

Lying back on the other bed, I laced my fingers behind my head and stared at the ceiling.

So that was what a night with a prostitute was like. One-night stands and unemotional sex were nothing new to me, but this had been different. A lot different. Even with a one-nighter that I knew wouldn't go any further, I'd always felt the pressure to at least pretend there was more between us than there was. With Sabian, I was free to lie back and enjoy the ride.

That's not to say sex with Sabian was cold or unfeeling. Far from it. With no pretenses of this extending beyond the allotted, prepaid time limit, there'd been no pressure. It was lust for me, business for him, and we both made damned sure I got my money's worth. I got my orgasms, he got his money, and we parted ways with what we both came for and no fear of unmet expectations on the other's part.

I sighed. Why couldn't it be like this with *every* guy?

Chapter Two

Sabian refused to be forgotten the next day.

While I sipped my morning coffee in my deserted kitchen, every last inch of my body ached, and my head was still light from the orgasms he'd given me. He'd made me climax more times than my previous boyfriend had over the course of several months. I had never considered myself to be multi-orgasmic, but Sabian either assumed I was or decided I would be.

He was incredible. Hell, of course he was. He didn't get paid for it because he was lame in bed.

Paid for it. I cringed. I still couldn't believe I'd resorted to a prostitute. More than that, I'd enjoyed it. And now I craved it. Hot sex, no bullshit, no one treating me like damaged goods because I had the audacity to have a couple of kids—what wasn't to love?

Well, besides the price tag, the stigma, and the regret that really wasn't regret. How could I simultaneously regret it and want so badly to do it again?

My smoker friends might be able to answer that question.

Pouring my second cup of coffee, I groaned and rolled my eyes. It wasn't an addiction. It was a onetime indulgence to blow off some steam. I'd gotten it out of my system, and that was that. And now that it was out of my system, it was time to get back to real life.

It was Sunday, which was the day my ex-husband and I traded the kids for the week. I spent the day getting everything done that needed to be, all the cleaning we would negate before the week was up, and I tried unsuccessfully not to think of Sabian the whole time. That evening, on my way over to Michael's place, my stomach was still a ball of guilty, self-loathing nerves.

I couldn't decide what bothered me more: that I'd done what I did with Sabian or that my love life had gotten so pathetic and frustrating that I'd even felt the need to resort to it.

Oh, well. There would be time to wallow in it later. Starting now, as I pulled into my ex-husband's driveway, I needed to switch on parent mode.

I rang the doorbell, and Carrie, my ex's wife, answered.

She smiled and stood aside to let me in. "Right on time, as always."

"Would you expect anything different?"

She laughed. "Not at all. Come on in. Michael's upstairs helping them get their schoolbags and everything together. They'll all be down shortly."

"No rush." I followed her into the kitchen. From upstairs came footsteps, voices, shuffling papers, and drawers opening and closing.

"Can I get you some coffee?" Carrie asked.

"Oh, no, I'm fine. Thank you."

She picked up her own coffee cup. "So how are things?"

"Same old, same old," I said. "Work, work, work. That place is going to send me into an early grave, I'm telling you."

Scowling, she nodded. "God, yes, I know the feeling. I'm starting to think meetings were invented solely to waste time and drive me insane."

"I figured that out the day they invented PowerPoint."

Carrie groaned. "Ugh, that program is the bane of my existence." She gestured toward the stairs with her coffee cup. "You know, Michael was at an awards banquet recently, and some guy broke out a PowerPoint presentation in the middle of dinner."

I blinked. "You're kidding."

"Not even." She sipped her coffee and set the cup down. "He said it killed every last person's buzz, so they all had to start drinking all over again."

"Maybe the guy had a deal with the bartenders, then," I said.

She laughed. "Maybe so." She started to speak again, but footsteps on the stairs turned both our heads.

Michael appeared in the kitchen doorway. "Hey, Jocelyn." He gestured over his shoulder with his thumb. "Kids are just about ready to go."

"I'm in no hurry," I said. "Carrie was just telling me about your death by PowerPoint at a banquet."

"Oh, God." He rolled his eyes. "That was some bullshit, let me tell you."

"Of course it was," I said. "That's why they were using PowerPoint to present it."

He chuckled. "Good point." He rested his hands on the back of one of the kitchen chairs. "So, kid stuff. Mikey's got tryouts for wrestling on Wednesday after school. Will you be able to pick him up?"

"What time will it be over?"

"Four thirty."

I nodded. "I may have to shuffle a couple of appointments around, but I think I'll be able to, no problem."

"If not, let me know," Carrie said. "That's my work-at-home day, so I can get him if you need me to."

"Okay, thanks, I'll let you know." To Michael, I said, "He turned in his paperwork from his physical, right?"

"Yeah, I made sure he had it in last week."

"Okay, good."

"Oh, and on the twenty-seventh, there's a father-son thing for scouts," he said. "It's a Tuesday, during your week. Do you mind if I take him, and we can switch another day?"

"Sure, yeah," I said. "I think I still owe you a day from when I took them camping a few months ago anyway."

"Do you?" He furrowed his brow, then shrugged. "I don't know, I can't keep track."

I laughed. "Well, you take him for the father-son thing, and we'll call it even."

"Sounds good to me." He glanced toward the stairs. "Let me go see what's keeping them." He left the kitchen, calling to the kids to tell them to get their stuff together.

There were a lot of things I could say about being divorced, but if I had to have an ex-husband, I was glad it was Michael. We'd both watched plenty of couples fight over their kids, nitpicking custody arrangements down to two-minute increments, and each pitting the kids against the other, and we'd both sworn not to do that to our children. If anything, we got along better now and were better parents like this than we ever were before we'd split. If one of them wanted to stay an extra night at Michael's one week or have a birthday party at mine during his week, we didn't make a big deal out of it.

Sex and dating as a single mom may have sucked, but I thanked God every day for such an easy, amicable parenting arrangement with my ex-husband.

"Hi, Mom!" Alexis, my seven-year-old, trotted into the kitchen, arms out.

"Hey, you." I hugged her. "Got everything for the week?"

She nodded. "By the door."

"Okay, good. Where's your brother?"

"I'm right here," Mikey, my twelve year-old said, shuffling in the way his sister had come. He offered a brief hug. Ah, the joys of a preteen. *Glad to see you, Mom, but don't get all mushy.*

"You both ready to go?" I asked. They nodded, so we all migrated from the kitchen to the front door. Hugs, good-byes, and my custody week began.

For the rest of the evening, the kids kept me occupied. It was "guess what happened at school this week" and helping with homework, figuring out extracurricular activity schedules, and packing lunches until it was time for them to go to bed. Once they were asleep, I settled onto the couch for a glass of wine and an hour or so of downtime before I went to bed myself, and what a surprise, my mind went right back to last night.

The pendulum swung back and forth between feeling guilty and wishing I could do it again. Having the kids in the house intensified the guilt, like I should have felt even worse because I wasn't just a single woman. I was a mother. I was supposed to be respectable or something.

Back and forth. Back and forth. I was reading too much into it, wallowing too deeply in something that wasn't a big deal. I was pretending it was no big deal when it was. I hated myself for doing it, and I wanted to do it again.

Eventually, I finished my wine and went to bed, pretending I stood a chance at sleeping without thinking about Sabian.

After I'd seen the kids off to the bus stop the next morning, I put myself together and headed off to work. One more step back into the world of being a responsible, respectable adult. I'd only escaped this life for a few hours on Saturday night, but it was surreal going back into it, whether as a parent or employee.

Come on, Jocelyn, get it together.

In the parking lot at the foot of my company's building, I took a deep breath. That night was supposed to relieve some stress, and it had. No sense canceling out the effect by stressing that it had even happened.

One more deep breath, and I was out of the car and on my way in to get to work. As soon as I walked in the door, Laura, my assistant, handed me a thick stack of phone messages and a thicker stack of files and forms for me to peruse, sign, correct, reject, scream at, shred, or forward. Fortunately, I had the kind of job that offered little downtime, which meant not a lot of time to think. Or dwell. Or wallow. Sabian was still on my mind but relegated to the back of it for now, because I had too much to do.

My desk was deceptively clear. Only my computer monitor, coffee cup, and office phone were allowed on the desk for any length of time. Paperwork was filed, my mouse and keyboard were underneath, and even pens lived in a drawer unless they were in use.

To clients and newcomers, I was organized and not swamped at all. Anyone who'd worked with me for any length of time knew it was an illusion, a sign not of my efficiency but of my neurotic aversion to clutter. With two kids at home, I could only keep the chaos under so much control, but here, in my office? Immaculate. It just gave the appearance that I wasn't nearly as busy as I was.

In spite of my brain taking occasional forays back to Saturday night, I hit my stride within a few minutes of coming through the door. Calls to return, e-mails to answer, meetings to attend, more meetings to schedule.

At one point, a glance at my appointment book sent my body temperature up a few degrees.

2:00—Meeting with Clark McEnroe.

Clark was one of those clients who had probably appeared in the impure thoughts of the majority of the women in this building. He and his good looks came in about once a month to discuss contract modifications or implementing his latest marketing strategies into his advertisements. When he did, it was no great secret that at least a dozen of my female colleagues would find reasons to be on my floor, milling around my assistant's desk or heading to nonexistent meetings. After he left, Laura always fanned herself with a file folder and commented that the powers that be must have been screwing with the air-conditioning again.

I'd long ago gotten the hang of getting through a meeting with him without stumbling over my words or throwing myself at him. That wasn't to say I'd never imagined hooking a finger under his tie and loosening it while accidentally pulling him closer. I could probably have been accused of the odd daydream about what he'd look like without that crisp white button-down. I *might* have entertained a fantasy or two about a long kiss. A *really* long kiss.

For the most part, I'd kept myself cool and professional around him, just like I did with any client.

When he sauntered into my office at two o'clock this afternoon, though, he didn't look like a man I could keep cool around. He always wore suits, but this one was tailored just right to showcase his broad shoulders and narrow waist. Maintenance must have changed some of the overhead bulbs over the weekend, because I didn't remember my office lights ever picking out the highlights in his hair or the blue of his eyes quite like that.

I'd also never noticed how long his fingers were. Long, fine fingers, every movement careful and precise even when he was doing nothing more than flipping through loose-leaf pages. While he read the latest proposed modification to his company's contract, he absently turned a pen over and over between his fingers, completely oblivious to all the things going through my head.

I shifted in my chair. My mind was like someone else's today, dragging Clark much deeper into my fantasies than ever before. Usually, I just caught myself wishing for a clandestine kiss or even a well-timed glance down the front of my blouse.

Maybe having my name on an escort agency's client list had freed my inner slut, and she wasn't the least bit ashamed of imagining Clark bending me over my desk or putting me on my knees to suck his cock. Forget having his shirt off. I wanted it rumpled, half-buttoned, and bunched in my hands. I wanted—

He suddenly looked up. "I think I like the new terms here, but I'm a little concerned—" He paused. "Did, um, did I say something wrong?"

"Hmm? No, of course not."

"Oh." He smiled, the hint of shyness making me tingle in places no professional woman should tingle when trying to stay in a client's good graces. "You looked like you were blushing a bit."

Me? Oh, nooo...

I coughed and made a dismissive gesture, then glanced at the vents above my desk. "They've been…screwing with the air-conditioners in here lately. Gets a bit warm." I cocked my head. "It's not too hot in here for you, is it?"

Yeah, that *didn't come across as a baited question.*

"No, I'm fine."

I cleared my throat. "You were saying, about the new terms?"

"Right. Right." He laid the pages on the desk, and while we went over his concerns, I didn't look at him like that again. Nor did it make my heart skip when he absently adjusted the knot of his tie.

Jocelyn, seriously, calm down.

"Looks like everything's in order." He slid all the paperwork back into its file folder. "I'll shoot you an e-mail if the powers that be object to anything."

"Sounds good." I rose and extended my hand. "Thanks for coming by."

"Not a problem." He shook my hand and smiled. "It was a pleasure, as always."

Yeah, you could say that. After some more polite small talk, I saw him out of the office.

Laura and I watched him through the tinted glass doors. I fanned myself with a file folder.

"Screwing with the A/C in your office this time?" she asked with a smirk.

I laughed. "Yeah, maybe."

"Don't blame you." She craned her neck to catch one more glimpse of him before he disappeared around a corner. "You're the one who gets to stare at him for an hour."

"Yeah, and try to maintain some semblance of dignity in the process," I said. "Not easy, my friend."

She put a hand over her heart. "Oh, I *ache* with pity for you."

We both laughed. Then I went back into my office and dropped into my desk chair. For a moment, I just stared at my desk, not even sure which task to jump on next. I had plenty to do and not enough time to do it, but damn if I could focus. I never had trouble concentrating at work, least of all because I was too busy entertaining racy thoughts about a longtime and respected client.

Except it wasn't just Clark. It wasn't the new guy in accounting who stopped into my office to pick up some papers and inadvertently wander through a fantasy involving chocolate sauce. It wasn't the pair of gorgeous models on their way down to photography after their combined presence made me seriously consider adding ménage a trois to my life's to-do list.

It wasn't *who* I wanted; it was *what* I wanted, and that was dirty, sweaty, unbridled sex. Lovemaking was fine and good, and someday, when a man came along with whom I connected enough for that to happen, fine. For now? I craved sheet-mangling, shoulder-clawing, headboard-pounding *fucking*.

I caught myself looking at the entire world around me in a different light, including my work environment. The stack of Xerox paper boxes in the supply closet would be uncomfortable as hell against my back or under my forearms, but wouldn't that be hot? I imagined myself getting fucked over the conference room table or right up against the pull-down screen, bathed in the multicolored glow of the projected death by PowerPoint presentation. My own office chair was the perfect height for a kneeling blowjob, and I absolutely did not spend a single second mentally measuring my desk's height in relation to my hips or those of any man who came into my office throughout the day.

"What the hell is wrong with me?" I muttered into the stuffy stillness of my office.

That was an easy answer. I'd tasted the kind of sex I'd been craving for the past few years, and now I wanted more. I wanted more, and it was still available for the taking. Money wasn't an issue. I would, of course, schedule it on a night when the kids were at Michael's. So why shouldn't I? No one knew about last Saturday, and they wouldn't know about the next one.

So much for taking the edge off. Obviously it wasn't a good idea to do it again, then. If it just made me want more and drove me to distraction, it was a bad idea.

A bad idea, but a hot one.

No no no. Once was enough.

By the time I left the office that evening, I was in dire need of ten minutes or so alone, which I didn't get until I went to bed at almost eleven. By the end of the week, ten minutes or so alone didn't cut it anymore, even twice a night. By Sunday evening, I'd run out of reasons why a repeat session with an escort was a bad idea.

So, after Michael came and picked up the kids, I made the call.

And I requested Sabian again.

Though he probably wouldn't remember me from Eve, he'd be familiar enough to me to ease some of my nerves. I told myself there was no sense putting myself through the same "what the hell am I doing with a total stranger?" anxiety this time if there was a way to alleviate it. That, and I knew he could satisfy me.

After all, Mama always said, if it ain't broke...

Chapter Three

The hotel's coarse wallpaper burned my shoulder blades, but Sabian fucked me too hard and too deep for me to give a damn. Every thrust meant more friction against the wall, but the only thing that mattered was his cock sliding easily in and out of my pussy, sending me closer to yet another orgasm.

I clawed at his shoulders, my fingers sliding across his sweat-soaked skin. I screwed my eyes shut and *tried* to cry out, *tried* to beg him to fuck me harder, but the air wouldn't move. Sabian certainly moved, though. Whatever it was he did with his hips, it was incredible. I didn't know if he twisted them somehow, or rolled them, or had sold his soul to the devil for the ability to get that deep at that angle and that speed and—

I whimpered and dug my nails into his shoulders, and damn if he didn't fuck me just a little harder *right* when I lost it, and the entire universe turned white. An unrestrained cry of ecstasy left my lips, and Sabian's breath caught. He thrust in as deep as he could, forcing himself into me so hard my back ground against the wall. Then he threw his head back and groaned.

In seconds, it was over, and I tangled my fingers in his sweaty hair while he panted against my shoulder. His arms shook. My legs shook. We tried to kiss, but we were both breathing too hard, so we gave up.

He let my legs down. For a moment, I leaned against the wall and held on to him, just trying to get my shaking legs under me. Sabian braced himself with his forearm. His eyes were closed. Drops of perspiration slid from his disheveled hair down the sides of his face and over his body, adding a sheen to his muscles and tattoos.

After a moment, he opened his eyes. "You all right?"

I nodded. "Just...shaking. A bit."

"Good. Means I did my job."

"I'm not complaining, believe me."

He kept an arm around me until I made it to the bed. While I tucked my trembling legs under the scratchy hotel blanket, Sabian stepped into the bathroom to take care of the condom.

Staring up at the ceiling, I let out a long breath. My back burned, my pussy tingled, my hips would probably hurt like hell in the morning, and this was exactly what the doctor had ordered. There'd be time for regret later.

Sabian came back into the room and got into bed beside me. I turned onto my side, and he draped an arm over my waist.

"You don't mind if we take a breather, do you?" I said.

"Not at all." He wiped some sweat from his forehead. "I could use one myself."

"Should I be gloating about wearing you out?"

He laughed. "Give me a few minutes, darlin', and we'll see who's worn out." Something told me he wasn't kidding.

"So, while we're catching our breath," I said, "I'm curious. And this might be a stupid question..."

"Try me."

"Do you have...regular customers?" *Please tell me I'm not the only repeat.*

"A few," he said with a nod.

"Really?"

"Yeah. It's not that uncommon." His palm drifted up and down the curve of my waist. "Makes my job easier sometimes."

"Does it?"

"I start remembering what she likes, that kind of thing."

"That actually brings me to something else I meant to ask you," I said. "Your company's site mentions all kinds of other services. What else do you do for your clients?"

He shrugged. "Depends on what she wants. Sometimes it's just an evening out; sometimes it's a night like this. Some women like to do a little role-playing once in a while."

"Role-playing? What do you mean?"

"Pretty much anything." His lip curled into a playful smirk. "Have you ever fantasized about fucking a customer, or a vendor, or even the guy who comes to install your cable?"

Me? Never. No way. Nooo. I cleared my throat. "On occasion, yes. Especially some of my clients."

"You're not the only one. I've had a few clients pay me to pose as *their* clients."

I cocked my head. "How does that work?"

"I'll go in like I've made an appointment," he said. "Go into her office, talk to each other like she's selling me her service, that sort of thing."

"And you fuck her?" I blinked. "Right there in her office?"

"If that's what she wants." He paused. "The rules are set up front. What we can and can't do, what she wants me to do, that sort of thing. Once I'm there, we act like I'm the one in charge." He winked. "The customer's always right, of course."

I shivered.

His hand stopped and his thumb made slow arcs along my side. "What's wrong?"

"Nothing." My cheeks burned. "Honestly, that's been a little fantasy of mine for a long time."

"Is that right?"

I nodded. "I get some attractive clients. Some *very* attractive clients. And sometimes..." Hotter still, my face burned, and I watched my fingers trace the tattoo on his arm. "I may have been known to fantasize about one or two of them taking the 'customer is always right' thing to...an extreme."

"More common than you might think," he said. "I've gone in for fake job interviews, client meetings, you name it."

I laughed. "You must be a pro at job interviews, then."

He snickered, sliding his hand from my side to my hip, where his thumb resumed those tantalizing arcs. "Yeah, except most real job interviews don't end with my cock in the interviewer."

"What a pity for the interviewer," I said, masking another shiver.

"It's an interesting part of the job." He chuckled. "It was kind of funny when I had an HR director bent over her desk once. Don't think she even noticed all the sexual harassment fliers, workplace code-of-conduct reminders, things like that, spread out all over the place."

I laughed again. "Oh, that must have been interesting."

"Yeah, it was."

"I could certainly see how a visit from you would break up the monotony of the workday."

"They seem happy." His eyes narrowed a little and he grinned. "Is that something you'd want to try?"

I pursed my lips. "Is this where you try to sell me additional services?"

"Probably." His cheeks colored. "Can't say I'm very good at that part."

"Really?"

He nodded. "I'm good at the services. The selling part? Not so much."

"Well, I'd offer to help with advertising," I said, still watching my fingers follow the curves and lines of his tattoo, "but that might raise a few eyebrows."

"I suppose it would. So you work in advertising, then?"

Shit. A personal detail. Oh well, it wasn't the only advertising firm in the city, and it wasn't like he knew my real name. "Yes, I do."

"Interesting job?"

"Probably not nearly as much as yours."

"Don't know about that," he said. "Mine's probably not as exciting and interesting as you might think."

"To be fair, you have sex for a living," I said. "I endure staff meetings and PowerPoint presentations."

He grimaced. "Okay, you're right; this *is* more exciting than that."

"Certainly more stimulating, anyway."

"Oh, yeah." He trailed a single fingertip from my side to my breast and drew a slow circle around my nipple. "Speaking of which, I do believe you're still paying for me to be here." Leaning in to kiss my neck, he murmured, "I should really make sure you're getting your money's worth."

I got my money's worth all right. Jesus, why couldn't I get sex like this without having to pay for it? Watching him pull his slate gray silk shirt over the pink stripes I'd left on his shoulders, it was oh so tempting to consider scheduling with him again. Or sampling that list of "other services" that had so piqued my curiosity.

Not tonight, though. Any more orgasms, and I'd have set off the hotel's fire alarm.

After he'd gone, I went in to take a shower. The water stung my back, reminding me of every place the wallpaper had chewed up my skin. I just closed my eyes and grinned to myself. For a night like this, some raw skin was a price I was willing to pay. An additional price, I supposed.

So he had regular clients. Women who came back for more, enough for him to know their names and remember their likes and dislikes. Was I really the kind of woman who'd do that sort of thing? Hell, what did I care what kind of woman did or didn't? I loved what he did to me. I could afford it. Why should I give a shit what anyone else might think if they somehow found out?

I let the water rush over my face. No, this wasn't something I could keep doing. Maybe every once in a while, when I really needed something to take the edge off. Then again, when Sabian took the edge off, it only served to raise the bar for any man who came along after him. Too much of a good thing, and I'd end up as picky as Kim when it came to men.

Kim, who used Elite Escorts quite often as far as I knew and hadn't had a relationship in years.

I had no regrets. Tonight wasn't a mistake, but I definitely couldn't make a habit of this. Tomorrow, I'd go back to normal dating, with all of its requisite bullshit, and eventually, I'd find what I was looking for.

I hoped.

Chapter Four

Dating sucks. That's all there is to it.

I couldn't decide which was worse: meeting people online or playing Dance Club Roulette. The former meant false advertising and creepy come-ons. The latter was the same, minus the misleading profile pictures and with the additions of alcohol and being way, way too close for comfort.

Occasionally, I met some great guys that way, but they usually turned out to have some sort of fatal flaw, such as an absolute and misguided certainty they were God's gift to women. Or a belief that kissing involved trying to wrap one's tongue around my tonsils. Once in a while, a lethal case of halitosis.

If they were still Mr. Perfect, they ran screaming for the hills when they found out about my kids. I guess I couldn't blame them. Not everyone wants to be a parent, and the prospect of an instant family was more than a little intimidating. Legitimate concerns or not, there was still nothing quite like being relegated to a category of dating prospects akin to dented soup cans, especially when some seemed less concerned with the kids and obligations as they were with what having two children had done to my body.

And I wondered why I'd resorted to a prostitute.

That had been fun, of course, but it was time to return to the real world and try to find someone more permanent and less expensive.

Between my kids and my job, the time I had available for dating and all its headaches was limited. At least my custody arrangement with Michael made things easier. We lived less than a mile apart, and since the kids went from one to the other every weekend, every other week was mine.

When the kids were at their father's, I tried to get out at least a few nights a week to meet people, plus an evening out with friends to commiserate about the results of our respective prowls. Those evenings with friends were a double-edged sword. On one hand, they offered some hope. Janie had finally found a great guy a year or so ago, and she'd recently seen him looking at the jewelry store inserts in the Sunday paper. Laura's latest boyfriend seemed like he might stick around for a while.

On the other hand, it could be a rather depressing reminder that Sarah, Vanessa, and I were all *still* single.

As much as it had its drawbacks, the online dating thing certainly had the advantage of being more efficient. I made far more connections than in person, and could tactfully bow out of awkward situations with a bland response or a blocked screen name. On a good week, I could "meet" a dozen or so guys and get two or three date nights out of it. With only every other week available for this, I tried to fit as many in as I could, especially since the vast majority didn't go beyond meeting for drinks or dinner.

In theory, meeting more guys meant more opportunities to click with someone, but usually it just meant an evening of conversation, maybe a good-night kiss on the cheek, and once in a while, a one-night stand or a second date. I was picky; they were picky. Such was life.

My dates were usually pleasant evenings, if nothing else. There were worse ways to spend a couple of hours than sharing some good wine and conversation, even if we never saw each other again.

As I dipped my toes back into the dating world now, I wondered again if an escort had been a bad idea. Every man's charisma and chemistry were measured against Sabian's. My entire sexual world had shifted beneath the weight of those two nights, and everything was filtered through Sabian-tinted lenses. The butterflies in my stomach had been spoiled and wouldn't even get out of bed, let alone give a half-assed fluttering, for anyone anymore. The mere *thought* of him, though, had them going wild.

In the month or so after my second time with him, I managed two one-night stands, and they both left me feeling cold. One came well before I even stood a chance at having an orgasm. While he snored away beside me, I let my hand and thoughts of a certain escort carry me into something resembling satisfaction.

The other was attentive and skilled, but the only chemistry we had was physical. I'm not even sure how we got into the bedroom. Conversation was stilted and forced, most of dinner was awkward, but then he'd kissed me in the parking lot, and what we lacked in conversation, we made up for in that kiss.

That night was hot, but disappointing in a way.

The fact was, I wanted Sabian. Sabian and his spectacular mouth. Sabian and his gold-foil-wrapped condoms. Sabian and his stamina that always outlasted the time I'd paid for.

I wanted him, but I had to be realistic. I couldn't just keep paying for sex to avoid the dating headache. If I wanted something in the long term, I had to stick my neck out there again and find someone. The occasional night with Sabian would only be salt in the wound, reminding me I only got that kind of sex if I bought it, and the price included waking up alone the next morning.

So that was why I sat alone at a table in an intimate restaurant full of couples, waiting for my date to show up. I looked at my watch. Eight fifteen.

Fifteen minutes after he was supposed to show up, and fifteen minutes before Sabian would have been arriving had this been that first night—

"Stop it, Jocelyn," I muttered into my water glass.

Oh, but that was a train of thought that wouldn't be stopped. While I wasted what precious little time I had for this, I could have had an evening of guaranteed orgasms without the need to put on a fake smile and pretend it was more than a one-night stand. Or, at the very least, I could have been certain of a knock on a hotel door at exactly eight thirty instead of twiddling my thumbs at a half-occupied table for two while the ice in my glass melted along with my patience.

I glared at the door, trying to conjure Bill out of thin air and determination. It didn't work. I gritted my teeth. Tomorrow night, the kids came back from

Michael's house. It would be another week before I could try this again, and I was *not* in the mood to be stood up. This guy was probably chronically on time to business arrangements. Seemed like that type was usually late to anything of lesser importance. Like dates.

Maybe if I'd hired *him for tonight...*

The air in the room changed as it had every time the restaurant door had opened, and just as I'd done every time, I looked up.

This time, I was rewarded with a newcomer who actually looked like his profile picture from the dating site. Right around six feet, athletic build, dark hair that was forgivably longer than it had been in the picture. He was twenty minutes late, but he'd arrived and hadn't lied about his appearance, so I'd let it go and see how the night progressed.

It didn't take him more than a few seconds to find me, and he hurried across the restaurant to our table.

"Jocelyn, I assume?"

"Yes." I stood, extending a hand. "You must be Bill."

"I am." We shook hands and took our seats. "I am so sorry I'm late. My son called and needed me to walk him through something on his math homework, and I didn't realize the call had taken me so long." He made a flustered gesture and shook his head. "And then I was in such a hurry to get on the road and get here, I forgot I hadn't put your number in my phone."

And with that, the man is redeemed.

"It's okay." I smiled. "Kids come first; I know how it goes."

At that, he released a breath and relaxed a little. "They do, don't they?"

"Always." I folded my arms on the table and leaned on them. "Mine have to call their dad for help on math homework too. It never has been my best subject."

"My son would do fine with it if he worked at it." He rolled his eyes. "Doesn't help that his mother coddles him when it comes to his schoolwork."

Ripping on your ex before we've even ordered. Lose two points.

"Oh," I said. "Well, I—"

"The thing is, the kid's sharp as a tack," Bill said. "If he'd put the effort in like his brother, he'd easily be a straight-A student."

"Maybe math just isn't his strong point," I said drily.

"Maybe not, but it's not as weak as he likes to think it is." He sighed. "My ex-wife is convinced he has a learning disability. The only disability he has is learning to sit down and study." He laughed. I didn't.

Ripping on your own kid. Disqualification.

At least he didn't spend the entire evening criticizing his offspring's every shortcoming, but he talked about his ex-wife more than himself. Though his profile picture matched his appearance, he'd left "ranting about the ex-wife's every imperfection" out of the hobbies-and-interests section. I tried to steer the conversation toward less incendiary subjects, but somehow she kept creeping back into it, along with her infidelities during their marriage, her inability to cook like his mother did, and the way her body was never the same after she had his children.

Well, aren't you just a prime catch, Bill?

This date couldn't be over fast enough, and after dinner, a promise to call, and a tactfully dodged good-night kiss, I resisted the urge to ask for his ex's phone number so I could have coffee and commiserate. Instead, I went home for a glass of wine that wasn't soured by unpleasant conversation.

Sipping my wine in the silent darkness of my empty living room, I closed my eyes. Not every date was like this, not every guy had the kind of deal-breaking flaws as Bill, but every one of them left me with this same empty, discouraged feeling. This teeth-grinding "what the fuck was the point of that?" frustration. Did it ever get better?

Michael and I had married right out of high school, and jumping into the adult dating world in my late twenties had been a rude awakening. One that hadn't presented me with a hell of a lot of hope. If I could connect with someone enough to even get a date out of it—meaning he didn't balk at the fact that I had children—then something happened, or didn't happen, to make the date a dud. Every date left me wondering why the hell I bothered anymore.

And lately, to frustrate me just a little more, every date, every good-night kiss cooling on my lips, every empty promise to call me, every one-night stand riding off into the sunset, had as its backbeat the rhythmic banging of a phantom headboard against a pastel wall beneath a bland watercolor painting.

Chapter Five

On Friday, one of my coworkers, Janie, caught up with me on my way out of the millionth staff meeting this week. She fell into step beside me in the hallway.

"You going out for drinks with us tonight?" she asked.

I shook my head. "Can't. I have the kids."

"Oh, damn," she said. "Well, we're all going out to lunch too. You want to go?"

I held up the thick stack of file folders in my hand and gave an apologetic look. "I'd love to, but I have to work through lunch today."

"Really?" She wrinkled her nose. "They loading you up that much?"

"That, and I've got a meeting this afternoon that's going to cut into my time to get all this crap done." I shrugged. "Such is life, right?"

"Well, as long as they're not making you stay late," she said.

"God, don't give them any ideas."

She laughed. "Okay, well, let me know when you're free one of these nights so you can go get trashed with us."

"Will do."

She stopped to wait for the elevator while I kept walking.

"How much did I miss?" I asked when I got to my assistant's desk.

Laura, my assistant, held up a delightfully thick stack of pink phone messages. "Phone's been ringing off the hook."

"Great." I flipped through the stack, skimming for anything urgent.

"Hey, I just noticed," she said. "You actually wore your hair down for once."

I brushed it off my shoulder. "Yeah, I was in too much of a hurry this morning to put it up."

"Looks nice."

"Thanks." I smiled. "Oh, by the way, I've got a meeting at two with a potential new client. His name is Mr. Hendricks. When he gets here, please let me know right away."

She nodded. "Will do."

"And it's a 'don't let anyone interrupt me unless the building's on fire' meeting," I said. "So, you know the drill."

"Hold your calls and barricade the door," she said, laughing. "Got it."

With messages and a shitload of work in hand, I went into my office and shut the door. I leaned against it, closing my eyes and letting out a breath. Days like this, I needed a break like nobody's business.

Breaks were for people with time, though, so I pushed myself off the door and took a seat at my desk to catch up on all the e-mails, voice mails, and handwritten phone messages that had avalanched in during the staff meeting. Yet another reason staff meetings were, in my completely humble opinion, worthless wastes of time.

But what the higher-ups wanted, the higher-ups got, so now I jumped in and got caught up. I ate lunch at my desk in between making and taking calls. I completely lost track of time and didn't even blink when my phone rang for the seven hundred thousandth time while I tried to finish everything else.

This time, Laura's extension lit up the screen. I picked up the handset. "Yes, Laura?"

"Mr. Hendricks is here for his appointment."

Already? Absently smoothing my shorter-than-usual skirt over the garter I'd never worn to work before, I checked the clock on my computer. Sure enough, it was two o'clock sharp.

"Excellent. I'll be out in a second." I hung up the phone and put away all the papers I'd been working on, restoring my desk to its bare, immaculate state.

On my way out of my office, I stopped with one hand on the doorknob. Deep breath. Deep, cleansing breath.

Then I opened the door, stepped out into the busy reception area, and my attention was immediately drawn to my waiting client.

Oblivious to the hustle and bustle all around him, he was the very picture of relaxed and casual. Legs crossed at the knees and hips twisted just slightly. Button-down shirt with the top button left open. Elbow on the armrest. One finger absently tracing the side of his neatly trimmed goatee. We made eye contact from across the room, and when he grinned, my nipples hardened.

He watched me come around to the front of Laura's desk, his eyes making a slow trek from my slightly low-cut blouse to my hemline, then down my legs. When he got to my shoes, which were a good inch and a half higher than I ever wore to work, he gave the subtlest nod of approval. Then his eyes flicked up and met mine.

"Mr. Hendricks," I said, exchanging a knowing look with him as I extended my hand. "Glad you could make it."

He rose before shaking my hand. "I hope I'm not keeping you from anything, Ms. Rhodes." My real name sounded like pure filth coming from him.

"No, of course not." I gestured toward my office. "Shall we?"

"After you."

I started toward my office, and Sabian followed. He kept a few feet between us, and when I looked over my shoulder, I did so just in time to catch him giving me a conspicuous top-to-bottom glance.

In my office, he was even less discreet, tracing my figure with his gaze before meeting my eyes again.

I grinned. He winked. I shivered.

It didn't matter if he meant it or if it was just because I'd paid him to do it. It had been too long since someone had looked at me that way, and damn it, I liked it.

"So, Mr. Hendricks." I couldn't help smirking at his false name. "What can I do for you?"

He raised his chin just enough to emphasize our height difference. "I don't know, Ms. Rhodes. What *can* you do for me?"

"The customer's always right." I folded my arms across my chest, and he looked down the front of my blouse in the same moment I surreptitiously pushed my breasts up. "You tell me."

"Hmm, well." He reached for my waist, and my suit jacket wasn't nearly thick enough to keep the heat of his hand from my skin. "I was thinking the company could use some different branding. Something with"— he watched his hand drift up my side—"smoother lines. Maybe some curves to catch people's eyes."

Willing my voice to be steady, which was not easy at all, I said, "I think that could be arranged."

"Do you?"

I gulped. "Just tell me how you want it, and I'll do it."

"Oh, I have no doubt about that." He trailed a finger down my side, over my hip, across my thigh. "And I don't want anything complicated. Simple, nothing too busy. I like things..." Leaning in close, stopping with our lips nearly touching, he whispered, "Tight."

I sucked in a breath, and Sabian laughed, letting his lip just graze mine before he pulled back. He walked around me. I stayed still, but my senses homed in on his every move, following him past the edges of my peripheral vision until he stopped behind me. I closed my eyes, listening, sensing, trying to guess where he'd touch me—*if* he'd touch me.

Fingertips landed softly on my shoulders, and I jumped, pushing against his hands.

"This okay?" The playful lilt in his question told me he knew exactly how okay this was.

"Yes," I breathed.

"Good." He gathered my hair and drew it back into a handheld ponytail. Hand over hand, he stroked my hair, not pulling enough to hurt, but tugging just enough to let me know he could make it hurt if he wanted to.

After a moment, he laid my hair over one shoulder. Then he held my hips and pulled me against him, and when he spoke, his lips brushed my neck.

"What do you think, Ms. Rhodes?" His soft goatee and softer breath tickled my skin. "Do you have what I'm looking for?"

I turned my head, bringing him back into my peripheral vision. "I guess you should find out, shouldn't you?"

"I guess I should." He cupped my jaw in one hand and craned his neck enough to kiss me.

Then he let me go. He walked around my desk and sank into my chair. The chair offered a halfhearted creak as Sabian got comfortable. Putting one ankle on his opposite knee, he beckoned to me. I came around the desk and faced him.

Leaning his elbow on one armrest, he thumbed his goatee. "Let's see what you've got, then." With his other hand, he gestured at me. "Take off your coat."

I shrugged it off. Sabian was in my chair, which was where I usually hung it, so just this once, my neurotic anti-clutter mind would have to deal with my jacket draped over the top of the file cabinet.

"I'd have you unbutton your blouse," he said. "But it looks like you've already gotten a head start."

I looked down. I'd deliberately left the first couple of buttons open, keeping it within the realms of office-appropriate while still giving someone like him, a few inches taller than me, a good view.

Looking at him again, I said, "Sorry to disappoint."

"Oh, you didn't disappoint." He traced his lower lip with the tip of his finger, and if I hadn't already been turned on beyond reason, that asymmetrical grin would have done the job. "You didn't disappoint at all." The same finger gestured at my blouse before returning to his lip. "Unbutton the next two."

Once I'd done so, he nodded with approval.

"I like it just like that. So I can see some, but not all." His lips curved into that devilish grin that was rapidly becoming familiar. "Leaves my imagination to fill in the rest."

"You've seen the rest," I said.

"Not with that bra, I haven't. Red lace looks good on you, by the way." He put his foot down and sat back, folding his hands over his belt buckle. "Come a little closer."

I did, stopping when our knees nearly touched. He gestured at my foot and beckoned with two fingers, so I put my foot on the chair beside him.

"Oh, now I like that." He ran the backs of his fingers down my shin. Looking up at me through his lashes, he said, "Nylons are *so* much sexier than fishnets."

"Are they?"

"Very much so." The flimsy layer of nylon created a whisper-thin barrier, a soft wall between us, rationing unhindered contact to only the rarest rendezvous between his flesh and mine. "So much easier to feel what's underneath."

He put his hand on my knee and let it slide down my calf. Trailing a fingertip along the thin leather strap over my ankle, he teased my skin until goose bumps rose beneath my stockings.

His other hand started on the inside of my ankle, drifting up the back of my calf to my knee. Then his fingertips slid along the underside of my thigh to the top of my stockings, and when skin met skin, I gasped and nearly pulled away, but his other hand kept a firm grasp on my ankle.

He looked up. "Something wrong?"

"No." I licked my lips. "Not at all."

"I didn't think so." He ran his fingers back and forth along the border between flesh and fabric.

Then he continued higher. His fingers found my pussy, and he looked up at me with a devilish grin. "No panties. Very nice."

"I had a feeling you'd—" I gasped when one fingertip made a light circle around my clit.

"You had a feeling, what?"

"That you'd—" One finger slipped inside me. "That you'd like—" Two fingers.

He clicked his tongue and shook his head. "Tsk-tsk. I expected you to be so much more articulate with your clients, Ms. Rhodes."

Oh, Jesus, I loved the way he said my name.

"I usually am," I said. "But my...clients... They don't..."

He crooked his fingers slightly, removing my ability to speak and very nearly doing the same to my ability to stand. "They don't what?"

"They..."

His thumb brushed over my clit. Then, eyes locked right on mine, he whispered, "They don't usually have their fingers in your tight, wet cunt?"

I whimpered and somehow, heaven knows how, managed to murmur, "No, they don't."

Sliding his fingers a little deeper, he said, "What a pity for them." He gave a quiet laugh that was nearly as dirty as everything he'd said thus far. "And for you, I'm guessing. You've been thinking about this all day, haven't you?"

No point in denying it, not when his fingers moved so easily inside me.

"Yes," I said. "I have."

"And I'll bet," he said, teasing my clit with his thumb, "you've been thinking up all different things for us to do during this little 'meeting.' Am I right?"

Guilty. As. Charged. "Oh, yeah."

"Maybe you've been thinking about me fucking you over your desk." He was almost whispering. "Tell me, did you imagine me laying you across it on your back? Or bending you over it and fucking you from behind?"

"I..." I sucked in a breath. Fuck, I couldn't speak. He knew exactly how to touch me inside, how to tease my clit, and I didn't have a clue how to work my own mouth right then.

He leaned forward and pressed his lips to the inside of my knee, the warmth of his touch through my stockings making my toes curl inside my shoes. "Or were you too busy imagining me putting you up against that file cabinet? Or up against your door, to see if you could stay quiet enough that no one on the other side would know what we were doing in here?"

I hadn't even thought of either of those options, and they were suddenly so, so tempting.

"Or maybe," he said softly, "you pictured me sitting just like this, holding on to your hips while you fucked me."

My knees trembled and my balance wavered.

"Put your foot down," he said.

Thank God. With both feet on the floor, my balance was better. A little better. As much as could be expected with Sabian's fingers still inside my pussy.

Without withdrawing them, he rose, pushing the chair out of the way with his foot. Then he guided me up against my desk. Leaning in almost close enough to kiss me, he whispered, "Do you want me to fuck you, Jocelyn?"

My first name sounded even dirtier, even more intimate, than any word that had ever left his lips.

"I..."

His fingers crooked inside me again, just enough to take my breath and balance away. I grabbed the edge of my desk with one hand, his shoulder with the other. Then he slowly withdrew his fingers, and as his hand broke contact with my pussy, I could finally breathe. Maybe even form a coherent thought.

Sabian didn't let that situation last. He seized my hair with his other hand, gripping it tight enough to hurt and make my nipples harden that much more. "I asked you a question," he growled.

"Yes," I breathed. "I want you to fuck me."

"I thought you might," he said and kissed me lightly. "I'm not sure I'm ready to fuck you, though."

His grip on my hair was tight enough to keep me from moving, which meant I couldn't look down to see what his other hand was doing. The metallic clink of his belt buckle clued me in, though, as did the sound of his zipper. My mouth watered. The way he held me now, he was one twist of his hand away from forcing me to my knees to suck his cock.

Yes, yes, please, I wanted to beg. As much as I wanted him inside me, I desperately needed to kneel in front of him and make him come.

"Tell me what you want," he said.

"I want..." I swallowed hard. "I want to suck your cock." I'd barely whispered, but I was sure everyone in the building heard, and I didn't care at all. I only cared that he'd heard me.

"Do you?" His lips almost touched mine, and the hand in my hair kept me from closing the distance enough for them to do so.

"Yes." I tried not to notice the way his shoulder moved, tried not to imagine what his hand was doing just beyond the lower edges of my peripheral vision.

"You want to get on your knees," he whispered, "right here in your own office, and suck my cock?"

"Yes."

"I thought you wanted me to fuck you." He dipped his head to kiss my neck, and both his lips and goatee against my skin made thinking nearly impossible. "Which is it? Do you want to suck my cock? Or do you want me to fuck you?"

"I…"

"I already know what's going to happen." His tone was caught in some spine-tingling gray area between teasing and growling. He raised his head and looked down at me. "But I want to know what you *want*."

I moistened my lips and forced myself to look in his eyes. "I want to…suck your cock."

"Do you?"

"Yes."

"Mmm, I love to hear that." He leaned in to kiss me. "Nothing quite like a woman who wants to get on her knees and do just that."

I shivered, my mouth watering with anticipation. I couldn't remember the last time a man had talked so dirty to me.

He kissed me lightly. Then, using only the hand in my hair, he turned me around and forced me over my desk. I had to bite my lip to keep from yelping from both pain and surprise, but somehow stayed quiet. He leaned over me, pressing his cock against me and pulling my head back so he could whisper in my ear.

"But I want to fuck you." His goatee brushed the side of my neck when he added, "Don't move."

He released my hair and stood. I didn't move. Couldn't have if I'd wanted to. Sabian had me turned on and bent over my desk in the middle of the day, and—

Oh, God. I never knew the sound of tearing foil could be so damned arousing. I gripped the other side of my desk, certain I'd melt the second his cock touched me. Closing my eyes, I held my breath as he pushed my skirt up over my hips.

"Jesus," he breathed. "I love the way your ass looks like this." He traced the edge of the garter over my hip. "Red garter, no panties, thigh-highs. You know exactly how to get to a man, don't you?" Then he leaned over me. He cupped my ass in one hand and whispered in my ear, "I can't tell you how tempting it is to leave a handprint right there."

I sucked in a breath and shivered beneath him.

"And I would." He kissed the side of my neck. "But someone might hear, so I'll just have to save that for another time, won't I?"

He didn't give me a chance to answer. It was impossible to speak or think or fucking breathe when his cock pressed against my pussy, into my pussy, sliding deeper, slowly, slowly deeper. That very first stroke was enough to turn my vision white, and each was more intense than the last.

I expected him to fuck me hard and fast, but he didn't. He took long, smooth strokes, and he made sure I couldn't move to encourage him to go faster. He leaned over me, resting his hands beside mine, using his body weight to keep me from moving. The edge of the desk bit into my hips, but I didn't care, not when Sabian's cock slid back and forth across my G-spot like that.

In theory, anyone in the building could have come through that unlocked door. They wouldn't, of course. No one dared walk in during client meetings, and even if they did, they'd have to get past Laura first. Still, just knowing anyone *could* have walked in at any second made this infinitely hotter.

Sabian stopped. When he withdrew this time, he pulled all the way out.

"Turn around," he said.

I pushed myself up and faced him. He grabbed my hair again and kissed me. Passionately, violently, like he knew I'd let him part my lips with his tongue, like he knew I'd let him draw my tongue into his mouth. He kissed me like no one had any business kissing anyone in this office, and thank God he held me upright, because his kiss melted my spine one vertebra at a time.

Still kissing me, he put a hand between my shoulder blades and laid me across my desk. His mouth didn't even stop when he reached between us to guide his cock to me, and we both moaned against each other's lips when he thrust in. My desk squeaked in protest beneath us and pens rattled in the drawers, adding a muffled metallic rhythm section.

He stood upright and slid his hand down my leg, drawing my knee up to his hip. He wrapped his fingers around my ankle and brought it up to his shoulder. He rested it there, pausing to kiss the inside of it, and even through my nylons, the warmth of his lips made my breath catch. Then he put my other ankle on his other shoulder.

That angle was amazing, but I wasn't prepared when he leaned forward just enough to roll my hips back. I gasped, screwing my eyes shut and clapping a hand over my mouth to muffle the delirious cry that almost escaped.

"Like that?" he asked with a grin in his voice.

I whimpered something close to a yes. Understatement of the decade. This angle. His cock. That rhythm. My G-spot. Oh, fuck.

"Touch yourself," he said. "I want you to touch yourself so I can feel you come."

I wanted to be embarrassed. Sure, I'd done this the first time we'd fucked, but I hadn't been able to see his face. He hadn't watched. He hadn't so brazenly told me what he wanted and why.

I wanted to be embarrassed, but more than that, I wanted to come, so I did as I was told. It barely took any contact at all to put me into orbit, so I tried to hold back. As much as I wanted to come, I didn't want this to be over quite yet.

I didn't have much choice, though. Between my own fingers circling my clit, Sabian's cock showing me exactly why my G-spot was where it was, and this whole hot, forbidden situation, I was an orgasm waiting to happen. A loud one too, so I bit the second knuckle of my index finger, digging my teeth in to keep myself quiet.

"That's it," he whispered, his thrusts punctuating his words. "Let yourself go. Jesus, your pussy is so tight when you—"

My orgasm took over, and I didn't hear another word. Trying to keep it quiet only made it more intense, as did Sabian's perfect, steady rhythm. I swore it went on for several minutes. Probably only a few seconds, but damn if it didn't feel like forever.

Finally, I exhaled and relaxed. Sabian slowed to a stop. I blinked a few times, staring up at the ceiling and letting my vision clear before I looked at him.

He bent to kiss me lightly. "Still feel like sucking my cock?"

Did I ever, and his grin told me he already knew the answer.

I nodded. Sabian pulled out, then eased my legs down and helped me up. Then he sat in my chair.

Nodding toward the floor, he said, "Get on your knees."

With pleasure. I went to my knees and went down on him, something I'd been dying to do since the first time we'd fucked.

The faint bitter taste of latex didn't last long, but the sweet smell of my pussy remained, reminding me with every breath that he'd been inside me. Not that I needed anything to remind me, not with the aftershocks of my orgasm still tingling at the base of my spine.

He ran his fingers through my hair while I stroked and sucked his cock. "Oh, fuck, I knew you'd be good at this," he whispered. "Just like that, baby, that's perfect. *Fuck.*" God knew how much of it was an act and how much was true arousal, but a hard-on didn't lie, and every time his cock twitched against my tongue, lightning bolts shot up my spine like he was still inside me.

He wasn't easy to accommodate, but I managed. The vague ache in my jaw was well worth every low groan he released whenever I *almost* deep-throated him. His breathing quickened with my strokes. Soon it was nothing but sharp, irregular gasps, each shallower than the last, and I gave him everything I had.

"Holy...fucking...oh God..." He drew in a rush of breath, shuddered, and his cock twitched once, then again. With no sound beyond a ragged exhalation, he came, and I didn't stop until the hand in my hair tightened enough to signal he'd had enough.

I rocked back on my heels while Sabian got rid of the condom. My hands still shook, as did my knees. How many times I'd fantasized about everything we'd just did, I couldn't say, and I wondered if I'd ever be able to walk into this office without getting pleasant chills. My work environment would probably never be the same.

"So that's how role-playing works," I said.

He nodded, running a hand through his hair.

"I can see why it's so popular." I laughed. "Now I'll always wonder what my colleagues are doing when they take a client in their office."

Sabian chuckled. We both stood and went about fixing our clothes. While we did, I couldn't help noticing his hands were almost as shaky as mine. *Of course they are. The man just got laid. Doesn't mean a damned thing.*

I wondered, though, as I buttoned up my blouse, what went through his mind when he did this. Did he enjoy it? Was it all just business to him? Was he numb to it after doing it for money for so long? Did he spend the whole time wondering if he'd left the stove on or if he'd taken last night's DVDs back to the video store?

I wanted to pick his brain. Ask a million questions. Find out how he actually felt about his job, what he was like when he was off the clock. That was one request he probably wouldn't fulfill. Role-play, sex, conversation, fine. Personal questions about the man behind the sex and satisfaction? Probably not.

Could be worth a try, though.

After we'd both straightened our disheveled clothes and hair, I said, "So, I'm curious. If I wanted to book you as an actual escort, how much does that run?"

He leaned against my desk. "Don't quote me on it, but I believe the agency's rate is three to five hundred a night depending on how long you'd want me to be there."

"I may have to give them a call, then." I paused. "What exactly does that entail?"

"Same as any session. You're paying for my time and company." His grin weakened my knees all over again. "Anything you want to do with that time and company is up to you."

"Maybe I'll have to set that up, then," I said. "You don't mind me requesting you by name, do you?"

He laughed. "Hardly."

Of course he doesn't, idiot. Every time you ask for him, his wallet gets thicker.

"Well, anyway," I said. "I should let you go. And I should get back to my real clients."

"Right, of course."

I smiled. "And thank you. I needed this today."

"At your service." He put a hand on my waist, and I rested my hands on his chest. His kiss was gentle but anything but quick. We both held on for a long, long moment, lazily exploring each other's mouths. The hand on my hip became an arm around my waist. My hands moved up his chest and snaked around the back of his neck. He touched my face, sending a tremor right through me. It had been *ages* since someone had kissed me like this. Tender, unhurried, like neither of us had anywhere to be or any reason not to just melt into each other. The kind of kiss that didn't say good-bye and didn't quite mesh with the conclusion of a business transaction.

As gently as we'd come together, we separated. Our faces just inches apart, we looked at each other, and for a few seconds, I forgot who we were and why he was here.

Then we both stiffened. Our eyes widened and we both stepped back. I moved too quickly and wobbled on my unusually high heels, but Sabian caught my arm. He kept a gentle grasp until my legs were beneath me.

"You okay?" he asked.

"Yeah, yeah, I'm fine." I brushed a strand of hair out of my face and laughed. "Not used to these shoes."

He glanced down at them. "I don't know how you girls don't bust your ankles wearing those things."

"You're telling me." I glared at my shoes, then shrugged, thankful for something to think about besides the way he'd just kissed me. "Some girls know how to dance in the damned things. I'm lucky I can walk."

"Well, awkward to walk in or not, they *are* sexy."

"Thank you."

He smiled. "You're welcome." Our eyes met again. He swallowed hard. I chewed the inside of my cheek.

Then he cleared his throat. "I, um, I should get out of here so you can get back to work."

"Right. I guess you should get back to work too."

"Of course." He kissed me again, this time keeping it quick and to the point.

Without speaking, we left my office and went back out into the lobby. I suppressed a grin when Laura conspicuously checked out his ass on his way past her desk, and I almost laughed aloud when two of the other girls stopped to not so subtly gawk. If they only knew.

Sabian stopped by the door and faced me.

He extended his hand. "It was a pleasure doing business, Ms. Rhodes."

"Oh, believe me, Mr. Hendricks," I said as I shook his hand, "the pleasure was *all* mine."

Chapter Six

At precisely the agreed-upon time, Sabian strode into the agreed-upon restaurant in a slate gray three-piece suit, and I nearly dropped my wineglass. Crisp white shirt, cranberry tie with matching pocket square, and he'd finished the whole ensemble with glossy black shoes and perfectly styled hair. My God, he looked like he'd stepped right out of a *GQ* ad.

He caught my eye and acknowledged me with a nod before weaving his way through the tables and waitstaff. He certainly fit in with the scenery. This was a five-star restaurant with a house string quartet playing softly in a corner while couples danced on a small dance floor. It was filet mignon and the finest wines, the kind of place where someone dressed like Sabian looked right at home. It was expensive as hell and way over-the-top, but since I was already spending five hundred dollars for several hours of his company, what was another hundred or two for good food and wine?

When he reached our table, I stood and he kissed my cheek.

"Wine?" I asked as we took our seats.

"Please."

I poured him some from the bottle I'd already opened. While I'd waited for him, my nerves and I had shared a glass, and it hadn't done a hell of a lot of good. The "what the hell am I doing?" and "why the hell am I here?" still repeated loud and clear in the back of my mind.

And the truth was, sitting here sipping wine across a silver and china-set table from Sabian, I didn't have an answer. I had no clue what the hell I was doing or why the hell I was here. Okay, I was desperate for some dinner-table conversation that wasn't just a game of mutual manipulation to convince the other we both wanted to proceed to the next step, whether that was sex or another date. I was here because I loved dates but hated dating.

It had nothing at all to do with curiosity about this total stranger with whom I'd shared three of the hottest sexual encounters of my life. It wasn't even remotely related to any kind of delusion that I could get to know him or that there was any point in doing so.

Even if I *had* been curious about him for a while, and now that he wasn't expected to "perform" for the time being, maybe I could indulge that curiosity.

I set my glass down and ran my fingertip up and down the stem. "So, am I allowed to ask you personal questions?"

"You're paying for this." A hint of a grin curled the corner of his mouth, making me shiver at the memory of what those lips were capable of. "You can ask me whatever you want. I can't promise an answer to everything, but you're welcome to ask."

"I guess I'm just curious about your..." I paused. "Line of work."

The grin didn't falter. "You know what I do."

"Well, true. But I guess I don't know much about...the business. You know, what it's like to be an escort."

Picking up his glass, he said, "What do you want to know?"

"Is Sabian your real name?"

"No." The single word wasn't terse or sharp, but just firm enough to let me know it was the *only* answer I'd get to that question.

"So, um," I said, thinking quickly, "the company you work for. How many of you are there?"

"Just the guys you see on the site," he said. "Eight of us total right now, plus the two girls who run the place."

"The madams?" I asked with a cautious smile.

He chuckled. "They hate it when we call them that."

"I get the feeling you call them that anyway?"

With a devilish wink, he said, "Oh, you'd better believe it."

"I'm curious, do—" I paused. "You really don't mind talking about what you do, do you?" I glanced around the restaurant. "Out in public, I mean?"

"Not at all. You're footing the bill, so anything you want to talk about is fair game." His glance followed the same trajectory mine had. "With some discretion, of course."

"Of course." Truthfully, I was more interested in him in particular, rather than his job in general, but I was too nervous to dive right into asking. Strange as it was, though, it was easier to convince myself to ask potentially embarrassing questions about his job that it was to ask the most benign questions about himself.

"Is it true you guys use, you know, pills?" I asked. "For performance?"

Sabian laughed. "Some do, yes."

"Do you?"

He shook his head. "Tried it before. Stuff makes my heart race and sometimes it makes it damn near impossible to come." Inclining his head slightly, he gave me a look that made my knees tremble under the table. "What you get is one hundred percent pure Sabian."

"Impressive," was all I could say.

He chuckled and took another drink.

I cleared my throat. "So, what kinds of things have you had to do?"

"Well, no one's ever asked me to do a donkey show, thank God."

"Would you if someone asked?"

"Hell, no." He swirled his wine. "Honestly, a lot of times, it's just like this." He gestured around the restaurant with his glass. "A date. A night out. A conversation."

"So, it's not just..." I hesitated.

Lowering his voice, he said, "No, it's not just sex. Usually it's sex or something close to it, though. One woman paid me two hundred bucks just to make out with her in the backseat of her car for an hour. Fully dressed, nothing below the belt, just kissing in her car."

"Really?"

He nodded. "I don't know what her story was. Didn't ask, and she didn't say much of anything the whole time. That was all she wanted, so that was what I gave her."

"Funny, I always thought this stuff was straightforward," I said. "Pay, fuck, leave."

"It can be." He ran a finger around the rim of his wineglass. "Just depends on what she wants."

"And, being out in a car like that, in public..." I raised an eyebrow. "It doesn't bother you?"

He shrugged. "Why would it?"

"Cops, for one thing."

Sabian made a dismissive gesture. "Oh, I'm not worried about them."

"Even though you're..."

"A prostitute?"

I nodded.

He smiled and shook his head. "The cops don't bother us. Worst thing they ever do is tell us to take it somewhere else."

"Seriously?"

"Yeah. They couldn't care less about escorts, to be honest, and even if they catch us naked in the backseat of a car or something, they rarely suspect we're anything other than a couple of lovers who didn't feel like going home yet."

I played with the leather corner of my unopened menu. "Hmm, now I feel kind of stupid for thinking you were a cop when we met."

"No, it's not stupid." He folded his arms on top of his own menu. "If you're not experienced with these things, it's something to be concerned about. The truth is, though, they'd have to be really, really bored to bother with us. If they're inclined to bother with any of us, they spend their time busting the streetwalkers."

"None of the male prostitutes?"

"Oh, they get busted too." He idly traced the gold-embossed restaurant logo on the menu cover with his fingertip. "But the cops aren't as concerned with call girls and escorts as they are with the streetwalkers. Those are the ones who tend to be involved with rather unsavory types. Like pimps and drug dealers."

"Not the case with escorts and call girls?"

"Can be. But there's usually less trouble with us, so they pretty much leave us alone."

"So, with that client, being out somewhere in her car," I said. "It doesn't bother you, riding around with a stranger like that?"

He shrugged. "It's no greater risk than going into her home."

"Ever had any dangerous situations?"

"Oh, a few." He gave a quiet laugh and dropped his gaze, watching his finger follow the embossed lines on the menu. "I've had three separate clients grossly misjudge when their husbands would be home."

My eyes widened. "That must have been uncomfortable."

"You could say that." He blew out a breath. "I only ended up meeting one face-to-face. The other two kept their husbands distracted while I got the hell out of Dodge."

"What about the one who met you?"

"It was exactly what you'd expect." Sabian laughed and folded his hands over the logo he'd been tracing. "He threatened to do all manner of things to me, mostly involving detaching my balls from my body or killing me." Sabian shuddered. "Then she started screaming at him, and while they were arguing, I took off."

I laughed. "Oh, that must have been an interesting story to tell the guys back at the agency."

"They've heard worse, trust me."

"Does it bother you, being with married women?"

Sabian sighed, his humor fading. "It's one part of the job I really don't like. But she's the client. It's not my place to tell her that dropping a few hundred bucks on a night with me might not be the best solution to an unhappy marriage."

"I guess we all have our ways of dealing with those," I said. "Counterproductive or otherwise."

He looked at me. The question was in his alarmed eyes, but I guessed it was professionalism that kept it from his tongue.

"I'm not married." I reached for my glass. "Not anymore, anyway."

"Sorry to hear it."

"Such is life." I shrugged. "So, tell me more about the things people ask you to do. If you're okay with that, anyway."

"Of course, it's fine." He leaned forward and kept his voice down. "It's not uncommon at all for clients to have us go as their dates to company functions. Christmas parties, that kind of thing."

"The imaginary trophy boyfriend?"

He nodded. "She gets to show off that she's got a man even though she hasn't had time to even think of dating." He sighed again. "A lot of times, she's a woman who works herself into the ground, has to keep up appearances, but barely has time to call the agency, let alone find a real date."

"I can relate to that," I said.

"It's sad, really," he said softly. "I have met a lot of lonely women this way. Present company included."

Neither of us spoke for a moment.

Then I cleared my throat. "So, these company function clients, are they escort-only, or do they get the whole package?"

"Depends on what she wants. For some? I'm just her date, and when the party's over, she sends me on my way."

"And others?"

He rested his forearms on the table, leaning closer to me and lowering his voice. "Well, let's just say one Fortune 500 CEO and I pretty much destroyed a very expensive dress in the back of a limousine."

"Lucky woman."

He raised his wineglass, stopping just shy of his lips. "Another asked her secretary to come back to the hotel room with us."

"Oh, really?"

He nodded, rolling a sip of wine around in his mouth for a second. "I probably should have charged her extra for that, but..." He shrugged, and his grin was almost sheepish.

"You enjoyed that one, didn't you?"

"I had fun that night. I won't deny it."

"Don't you usually have fun with it?" I paused. "Or, at least enjoy it on some level?"

"Sure, but it has its moments. And it *is* a job."

"An interesting one, that's for sure."

Laughing quietly, he said, "It can be, yes."

I tapped my fingers on the stem of my wineglass, not sure if I wanted to take a sip or not. "But do you like what you do?"

"It beats the hell out of waiting tables or holding down a desk." He paused, grinning behind his glass. "Though I have, on occasion, been asked to hold down a desk."

I squirmed in my seat. "That's true, you have."

He winked and set his wine down. "Anyway, yeah, I like what I do."

I decided I needed that sip of wine after all. As I picked it up, I said, "I always heard prostitutes were treated like shit. Seemed like everything I ever read or saw in the movies, they were getting beaten, assaulted, whatever."

"It happens, but not usually with escorts. Not in this city, anyway." He clasped his hands together beneath his chin. "Fortunately, I work for an agency that sees the safety of its employees as equally important as the safety of the clients. We're not required to see a session through if it gets dangerous."

"Danger aside, does anyone ever treat you badly?"

"Occasionally," he said. "But you get that in any service industry. To be quite honest, I took more abuse in a given month slinging coffee in college than I ever have as an escort."

"Shows how much I know, I guess," I said. "Do you ever get male clients?"

"The agency does," he said. "But I don't. Some of the guys service both men and women; some are one or the other. Just women for me. If I'm requested for a three-way, it's always one where we focus on the woman only."

"And if she decided in the middle of it that she wanted you and the other guy to play with each other?"

Sabian pursed his lips. "If a client asked for it, then..." He shrugged.

"Just wouldn't be your thing?"

He shook his head.

"Do people ask you to do, like, kinky stuff?" My own question sent an image of Sabian, leather clad and smacking his palm with a whip, through my mind. *Price check on aisle five, please?*

"Sometimes," he said with a single nod. "I won't take on a client who's into bondage or pain, that kind of thing, though. I wouldn't know what I was doing, and I'd be afraid of hurting someone."

So much for that idea, damn it. "That makes sense, I suppose. Anyone ever try to hire you guys for bachelorette parties?"

"You mean as strippers?"

"That or anything else."

He laughed. "I never do bachelorette parties. We get calls occasionally, girls looking for strippers. We're a bit too expensive for most, and hey, I can dance, but not like that."

I raised an eyebrow. "You can dance?"

"I can hold my own."

I glanced at the dance floor. "So, does that cost extra?"

"It most certainly does not." Sabian stood and held out his hand.

This had to be a dream. A gorgeous man, a top restaurant, and he was willing to dance?

Oh. Right. I'd paid for this. As he led me out to the dance floor, I wondered if this was yet another reason going out with him like this wasn't such a good idea. If anything, it would probably just depress the hell out of me because the only way I could get this involved swiping my credit card.

Oh well. I'd paid for it, and I would enjoy the hell out of it.

"Just so you know," I said, putting a hand on the shoulder when we got to the dance floor, "I haven't danced in ages."

"Don't worry about it." He put a hand on my waist. "Just follow my lead."

"Simple enough," I said. "That's what I've done every time we've met."

He smiled. "Then this will be easy."

"Easy for you to say." *Forget dancing. I'm lucky I can walk when I'm looking at you like this.*

"Just trust me."

He wasn't kidding. The man danced like he fucked: perfect rhythm, flawless execution of every step, and my body followed. When another couple got in our way, Sabian just changed our course, and we glided right past the pair who wasn't so light on their feet.

"You really are good at this," I said.

His cheeks colored, and he laughed shyly. "Part of the job."

"Does it ever..." I paused, chewing the inside of my cheek, looking around in case any prying ears were too nearby. "What you do, does it ever bother you?"

"Not really." His eyes darted to my left, probably making sure there was enough room between us and another couple. "Some of the guys have a tough time with it. Some don't last more than a few months or even a few weeks. Me? It doesn't bother me all that much. It's business. Nothing more."

"It doesn't bother you that you're selling yourself?"

"I'm not selling myself," he said matter-of-factly. "I sell a service, use my body to give that service." His fingers curled against the small of my back, drawing me closer to him. "And afterward, I leave with just as much of myself as I came in with."

"Interesting way of looking at it."

"And if you think about it, it's really not that different from the games people play to get laid," he said. "Particularly if the roles were reversed."

"What do you mean?"

"Damn near everything people do is to get sex or money. I use one to get the other, just like everyone else." One corner of his mouth rose slightly. "Look at what you and I are doing. We both know what the deal is. You're buying dinner, paying me, and in exchange..." His eyes darted around the room, and when they met mine again, he lowered his voice. "In exchange, I'm yours for the night." Abruptly, he released my waist and raised my other hand to spin me. When my back was to him, he wrapped his free arm around me and let his lip brush my ear when he whispered, "Now, flip the gender roles and remove the business side of it. Instead of a few hundred dollars for the night, make it dinner out, a bracelet, an expensive flower arrangement."

I gulped. "I hadn't thought of it that way."

He turned me around and put his hand on the small of my back again, and I didn't miss the fact that we were even closer together now.

"Most people don't think of it that way," he said. "If anything, this is a more honest approach. We both know all of this"—he nodded toward our table—"is currency, and we both know what that currency is buying. Everyone else just fools themselves into believing they're doing something different."

Part of me wanted to get righteously indignant and defensive, angrily retorting that I had *never* done such a thing, that I'd only been on the paying side of an agreement like this. But another part of me—probably the same part that had hired him in the first place—couldn't argue. Maybe the whole dating routine *was* just nicely dressed prostitution.

"So why do you do it?" I asked. "For the sex or the money? Or both?"

"The money," he said simply. "The pay is great, and with the economy being what it is, quite frankly, I'd be stupid to give it up."

"That much I can understand," I said. "I think the money's all that keeps most people going to work every day. How did you—" I hesitated. "You really don't mind me asking, do you? I feel like I'm giving you the third degree."

"No, not at all." He smiled. "As long as it's not boring you to tears."

"Hardly."

The string quartet finished their piece, and while the rest of the restaurant patrons quietly applauded them, Sabian and I went back to our table.

With a fresh glass of wine in hand, I said, "I'm curious, how did you even get started doing this?"

"I needed the money." He topped off his own glass and set the bottle aside. "I'd just gotten laid off, and a buddy of mine from college had done it for a while, so I gave it a try. The thing is, the longer I do it, the more difficult it is to quit."

"You like it that much?"

He shook his head. "It's not that. I mean, I do like it, don't get me wrong, but it's when I go to apply for another job that it can be a problem. My work history for the last few years is legit and legal, at least on the surface, but any idiot can do a Google search of the agency's 'legit name' and figure out where I really worked and what I did."

"True. So, what would you be doing if you weren't an escort?"

"Same thing I do now. I'm an artist. That just doesn't pay the bills quite as well." He exhaled. "I can spend a month working on a painting and sell it for a few hundred bucks if I'm lucky. Or I can spend a few hours with a lonely woman and make five hundred." He paused. "My design work pays more than the paintings and stuff, but it's sporadic and not quite enough to keep my head above the water."

"Starving artist?"

"Pretty much. And really, what I do isn't a bad living at all. I'm not ashamed of it, I make good money, and my clients know exactly what they're getting."

"I never thought about this line of work as being an honest living," I said. "But I'm starting to wonder."

He laughed softly. "Well, it's not honest in the sense that it's not entirely legal, but I pay my taxes like everyone else."

"What's it like when you actually, you know, get involved with someone? Does this change how sex is for you?" I paused, cringing. "I'm sorry, that was too personal. You don't have to answer that."

"It's okay," he said. "Quite honestly, most people are too wrapped up in being appalled by what I do to even consider I might ever have a real relationship, never mind how my job might affect it." He smiled, and I swore he looked a little shy. "So I don't mind."

"Oh. Okay." I swallowed. "So, do you have relationships?"

"I've had a few," he said quietly. "And to answer your question, my job doesn't change what it's like at home. There's a difference between having sex and making love."

"I wouldn't know," I muttered into my wineglass.

He furrowed his brow. "Oh?"

"If I was making love with anyone, I wouldn't be paying for sex." My cheeks burned, and I glanced around the room, certain I'd just said that much too loud. Then I looked at him. "No offense, of course."

He chuckled. "None taken."

I started to say something else, but my phone vibrated, startling me. "Crap, I'm sorry. Give me a second." I took it out of my purse. Thankfully, it was Janie, probably checking to see if I wanted to go out boozing with the girls tonight. I switched the call over to voice mail and shoved the phone back into my purse.

"Sorry about that. I hate having to leave that thing on. In case my..." I hesitated, cursing the flush of heat in my cheeks. Lowering my voice, I went on, "In case my kids call."

"Don't be sorry." He smiled. "If your kids need to reach you, they need to reach you."

"I just hate having my phone go off when I'm out with someone, and especially on a—" I paused, laughing softly when my face burned even hotter. "I guess I forgot this wasn't a 'normal' date."

"What difference would that make?"

"Well, most guys hear about the kids and suddenly remember I'm damaged goods."

Sabian tilted his head a little. "Is it really that difficult for a single mom to meet someone?" He paused. "I don't mean that sarcastically. I mean, I really don't know what it's like for a single mother on the dating scene."

"Oh, meeting people is easy." I sighed. "It's getting anywhere beyond that that's difficult."

"How so?"

"If I just want a one-night stand, and sometimes I do, it's just as much headache as it is for everyone else." I sipped my wine but didn't set the glass down. "If I want something more? Then it gets complicated."

"I guess that makes sense," he said. "You'd think there were more guys out there who are fine with kids."

"Oh, yeah, a lot of guys say they're fine with kids. When my kids were little, all I met were men who interacted better with older kids. Once my kids were older, it was all guys who wanted to be a part of their lives from the beginning. I can't fucking win." I sighed. "I mean, I understand if a guy doesn't want to be an instant father. Being a stepparent isn't easy. My ex-husband's wife has had a pretty tough time with it herself. But damn if it doesn't make dating a royal pain, especially when a guy is convinced having kids has probably ruined my body, so—" I stopped, shaking my head. "I'm sorry, I'm rambling."

"You're fine," he said. "I assume all of that is why you decided to use an escort?"

My cheeks burned, and I nodded. "Pathetic, I know."

"No, I don't think so." He folded his arms on the table in front of him. "I told you, I meet a lot of lonely women in this business. The ones who work too hard, single moms, you name it. I don't think it's pathetic. I just think it's sad that women are driven to this."

"But you don't mind cashing in on it?" It came out with more bitterness than I'd intended, and I cringed when his face colored and he dropped his gaze.

"Fuck, I'm sorry," I said. "That was totally out of line. I'm—"

"It's okay." He met my eyes and smiled, though it was halfhearted. "In a way, yes, I'm cashing in on it. But I'm not out to exploit women who are driven to this. They need sex and company. I need money. You scratch my back, I'll scratch yours."

"I know, and I didn't mean that." I managed a laugh. "I guess I get a little bitter sometimes, and it can get the best of me."

"Understandable." He sipped his wine. "How old are your kids?"

I smiled. "Alexis is almost eight, and Mikey just turned twelve."

"Wait." Sabian blinked. "*You* have a seven- and twelve-year-old?"

I nodded.

"Wow." He smiled. "I wouldn't have guessed, honestly."

Rolling my eyes self-consciously, I said, "Is flattery part of tonight's package?"

It was his turn to blush. "No, I meant it. Honestly, I'd have said you were in your midtwenties."

"Not quite." I laughed. "I'm thirty-four."

His smile was both sexy and sweet as he said, "I never would have guessed." He laid his hand on the table, and I put mine over his.

"What about you?" I asked as his fingers moved back and forth along my wrist.

"Twenty-nine."

"And how many of those years have you spent in this line of work?"

"Three." He teased goose bumps to life on my forearm with his fingertips.

"Still not tired of it?"

He chuckled. "Oh, like I said, it has its moments, believe me."

The waitress came up to the table. "Are you ready to order?"

I looked at the menu, which still lay closed beside the wine bottle. I hadn't even thought about what I wanted to eat, and now that I did, nothing appealed to me. To Sabian, I said, "You know, I'm not really all that hungry after all. Do you have any objections to getting out of here?"

"Not if that's what you want to do." He raised his eyebrows. "You're calling the shots."

"So if I said I just wanted to go walk off this wine for a while, you'd be game for that?"

He drained his own glass and set it down. "Absolutely."

Chapter Seven

On the way out of the restaurant, Sabian offered me his elbow. I took it, and we must have painted a convincing picture of a couple just strolling down the sidewalk.

All the way to the waterfront a few blocks away, we didn't say much. I had hoped getting out of the restaurant would give me a chance to breathe, to take in some of the fresh cool air coming in off the bay, but all it did was unsettle me. Walking together, a phantom handprint on my waist from the dance we'd shared—this wasn't what he'd agreed to do. The safe confines of plans and a restaurant had switched to improvisation and outdoors.

This wasn't part of the deal tonight. Dinner, hotel room, good-bye. That was the deal.

I muffled a cough. "So, is this a normal part of your job?"

"There really isn't anything that's *not* normal, to be honest." He glanced at me and smiled. "I just go with it."

"Expect the unexpected?"

"Every night."

We walked in silence for a few minutes, following the boardwalk that overlooked the bay. Water lapped at the rocks below us, and the wind ruffled leaves on nearby trees. It was a cool night, so there weren't many people out and about beneath the harsh streetlights dotting the winding shoreline. We were completely out in the open, yet alone enough to grant more privacy than at our intimate table at the restaurant.

Still, I kept my voice low when I finally broke the silence. "Can I ask you another personal question?"

"Sure."

I hesitated, then looked at him. "What *don't* you like about being an escort?"

He was quiet for a long moment. I wondered if perhaps I'd dipped into the realms of too personal. Before I could retract the question, though, Sabian said, "The secrecy loses its novelty. Having to make up stories for why I have to bail on get-togethers, not being able to just be honest about what I do."

"I can imagine that gets old."

"Yeah, it does." As one, we stopped. I lifted my hand off his elbow, and he leaned against the metal railing. Without looking at me, he took a deep breath and went on. "And some people wouldn't believe it, but the sex has a certain amount of stress attached, and that can get old."

"Stress? What do you mean?"

He looked out at the water. "It's funny, a lot of people look at a job like this and think, 'how difficult could it possibly be?' But think of it this way." He turned to me. "You know how when you're with someone new, and you have to figure out all the things a new lover likes and doesn't like?"

I nodded. "Sure. That's half the fun of a new lover."

"It is, but I have to do that every single night. I know, I know, rough life. But it's…" He trailed off.

"Sort of like putting on the game face for a first date over and over and over," I said. "I guess I can see how that would get exhausting."

"Yes, exactly. Still beats the hell out of slinging coffee, though," he said with a soft laugh. "And at least I usually don't have to be at work at four in the morning now."

I grimaced. "That's a definite plus. I don't do early mornings."

"Neither do I. As far as I'm concerned, there shouldn't be two four o'clocks in a day, you know?"

"I am so with you on that." I wrinkled my nose. "Was one of my least favorite parts of having small children."

"Oh, yeah, I didn't even think of that." He looked at me with a playful scowl. "Inconsiderate beasts, waking you up at all hours of the night."

I laughed. "You don't know the half of it."

Our eyes met, and we both fell quiet again. The background noise of leaves and waves crescendoed to reach the foreground, filling the silence between us to remind me with each rustle and ripple that our conversation had fallen away. What did it matter, though? We were here for some superficial interaction and some scorching hot sex. Wasn't like we needed to keep up appearances and pretend this was a real date.

Are we pretending?

Before that thought had a chance to make my heart skip, Sabian looked at me. "It's funny, most people aren't interested in this stuff at all. I have sex for a living, and that's all anyone wants to see."

"I'm just curious about it. I hope I'm not prying."

"No, not at all." He looked at the pavement at our feet and swallowed. "To be honest, it's kind of nice to talk to someone who isn't busy passing judgment on me."

"I won't lie," I said, almost whispering. "I had my preconceived notions. But I'm starting to see that maybe they weren't all that accurate."

His eyes flicked up to meet mine, and the faintest hint of a smile brightened his expression. "Most people aren't willing to let those notions go."

"Most people haven't spent an hour or two picking a prostitute's brain, I guess."

The smile became a subtle laugh. "I suppose not. But then, I haven't met too many people who'd care to."

"Their loss."

Once again, silence settled in, and the wind and waves moved in to occupy it. And once again, it was Sabian who spoke first.

He took a deep breath. "You want to know what I really hate about my job?"

My heart beat faster, though I couldn't say exactly why, and I licked my dry lips before I said, "Sure, yeah."

He looked out at the water again. "In some people's eyes, I may as well be a registered sex offender of the most dangerous kind. If friends and family found out what I am, they'd probably move heaven and earth to keep me away from their kids."

Guilt gnawed at me. Before tonight, my first reaction would have been to get and stay between him and my kids. But before tonight, as much as it made me feel like a horrible person to admit it to myself, I'd never thought of a prostitute as being so...human.

He went on. "My biggest fear is someone accusing me of..." He trailed off, letting the shudder finish the thought. "God, I'd never hurt a kid—I'd never hurt anyone—but people have their beliefs, and they want to protect their kids." He sighed. "So I just make sure I'm never alone with my nieces and nephews or anyone else's kids. Not even for a few minutes."

"That's so sad that you have to do that."

He nodded, looking at the pavement instead of me. "Not much choice, I'm afraid. It's stupid, really. I get paid to have sex with adult women. How that translates into wanting to mess with kids is beyond me." He shuddered again. "But several of the guys I work with have told me very emphatically that accusations like that can and do happen."

I exhaled. "Wow. I mean, I understand being protective of your kids, but..."

Sabian nodded. "Yeah, exactly."

"Do you want kids of your own?"

"Eventually." Then, with a hefty and unexpected helping of bitterness, he added through gritted teeth,

"Assuming I can ever find a woman who's willing to have them with someone like me."

I blinked. "Oh?"

He grimaced and made an apologetic gesture. "I'm sorry, that was unprofessional. I—"

"It's okay." I smiled and put a hand over his on the railing. "This isn't an employee evaluation." He met my eyes, and we shared a quiet laugh. Then I said, "I never really thought about how a job like this would affect the rest of your life."

"It does, believe me."

"So how does it affect relationships?" I asked. "I mean, do you date much since you started working for the agency?"

"A little. Relationships don't last long in this business."

"I sometimes wonder if they last long at all," I muttered. "I haven't had one last longer than six months since my divorce."

"Neither have I."

"You're divorced?"

He nodded.

"Sorry to hear it."

"Such is life," he said.

Neither of us spoke for a moment.

"So what happened?" I asked at last. *How personal will you let me get?*

He was quiet for a few long heartbeats. Then, "We were too immature, and we didn't know how to be married. We both screwed up enough times there was no point in trying to keep it alive."

"Screwed up? In what way?"

"Lying to each other, which was usually lying by omission. Not cheating or anything, just not talking to each other about things that were bothering us." He took a long, deep breath, and his eyes focused on something in the distance. "Then we stopped talking at all and finally called it quits." He looked at me. "What about you?"

"Hmm?"

"Your marriage? What happened?" He paused. "If it's not too personal."

"Not at all," I said. "You showed me yours. I can show you mine." We both laughed halfheartedly again. As my laughter faded, I said, "We just neglected ours. We were both juggling graduate school while our son was really young. Spent a lot of time and energy stressing about money, the baby, that sort of thing. Then we both graduated, got good jobs, didn't have to worry about money as much anymore, and our son was old enough he didn't require the same constant attention." I looked out at the water with unfocused eyes. "About the time we realized we'd left our relationship in the dust, my daughter came along rather unexpectedly, and we just weren't in a place where our relationship could handle adding another baby to the mix." I exhaled. It still killed me to think about how Michael and I had buckled, and sometimes I still wondered if we might have made it had we been more patient, more mature. I swallowed. "So we split."

"How long have you been divorced?" he asked.

"Seven years. You?"

"Five." He exhaled sharply. "Man, sometimes it's hard to believe it's been that long."

"Tell me about it. Think you'll ever get married again?"

"Maybe. Just like with having kids. Depends on if I ever meet a woman who's willing to look past what I am." He looked at me. "What about you?"

"Same. Haven't had much luck yet, so color me a bit pessimistic."

"I suppose that can be complicated," he said. "From a guy's perspective, going from a bachelor to a stepfather is...intimidating."

"I know." I sighed. "The thing is, I'm not looking for a father for my kids. They have a father, and I'm not out to replace him. Of course whoever I'd marry would still be a father figure to them to a degree, but half the guys I date seem to think I'm looking for someone to completely fill Michael's role."

"Your kids have a good relationship with their dad, then?"

"Oh, yes," I said. "Michael's a wonderful father. We just sucked at being married to each other."

"I know that feeling," Sabian said softly. "My ex would have been an awesome mom. We just screwed up our marriage before we got that far." He laughed quietly, and I couldn't tell if he sounded sad or bitter. "Guess it's a good thing we did. I can't imagine having kids in the middle of it."

"Nasty divorce?"

He nodded. "Very. God, that was hell. I couldn't believe we'd let ourselves get to that point."

"Yeah, I understand that."

"I didn't go into my marriage lightly," he said, "and I felt like a failure when we didn't last."

"I know the feeling."

We both fell silent again.

"Out of curiosity..." I chewed my lip, still wondering how personal was too personal. Finally, figuring he could opt not to answer, I said, "When you do date, do you tell women up front? About your job?"

"I don't necessarily tell her within five minutes of meeting her," he said. "But I definitely tell her before I sleep with her." He said nothing for a moment. "I could never lie to a woman about this. If she trusts me enough for a long-term relationship, then she deserves the truth. And even if it's just a short-term thing, I owe it to any woman I sleep with." He paused. "I mean, I'm clean. Every one of us gets tested constantly for everything under the sun, and we always take precautions. But still, she has a right to know."

"Have you ever thought about giving it up?"

"I've thought about it," he said, almost whispering. "But regardless of what people think about what I do, I still have to eat. Some of the guys moonlight. They have other jobs, so they can take this job or leave it. I don't make nearly enough money with my other job to pay the bills."

"I suppose that would make things tricky with a relationship, then."

"Yeah. And really, it wouldn't make much of a difference if I quit."

"How do you mean?"

"Think of it this way," he said. "You'll always be a mother. Even when your kids are grown and gone with families of their own, you'll always be a mother." He met my eyes. "And to most people, I will always have been a prostitute. Even if I quit tonight and never took another cent for sex again, it'll always be there in my past." He shifted his gaze away, and when he spoke again, some of the earlier bitterness seeped back into his tone. "I will always be, in a lot of people's eyes, a whore."

"Wow, I hadn't thought about that," I said.

He gave a sniff of quiet laughter, and this time it was undeniably bitter. "Guess we both know what it's like to be damaged goods, don't we?"

"Yeah, I guess we do."

Sabian let out a breath. Then he shook his head. "I'm sorry, Jocelyn. This isn't what you paid for."

"I paid for an evening of company and conversation, didn't I?"

He pursed his lips. "Yeah, but probably not a depressing conversation about exes and that kind of thing. This is supposed to be about you. Talking about the things you're interested in."

"And right now, I'm rather interested in the fact that we have more in common than I thought."

Again, our eyes met.

Almost whispering, he said, "Yeah, I guess we do have a few things in common."

I forced a halfhearted laugh. "The escort and the single mom. Who'd have guessed?"

He shrugged, a hint of a smile tugging at his lips. "There aren't too many people who'd admit to having much in common with someone like me."

"Something tells me that's only because they don't know anything about you."

Sabian swallowed hard. Without a word, he reached for me, but not with the confidence of a paid prostitute who knew what he was doing. His hand approached my face slowly, tentatively, and when his fingertips brushed my cheek, we both took sharp, startled breaths. His other hand slid around my waist, and I put my arms around him. Out here in the cool evening air, the warmth of his body against mine was more pronounced than it had been when we'd danced earlier.

"I have to tell you," he said. "Whoever said you were damaged goods, they didn't have a clue what they were talking about."

I traced his goatee with the backs of my fingers. "Likewise."

For a long moment, we just looked at each other in the stark light. Then he leaned in closer. Our foreheads touched. His fingers trembled against my cheek. I lifted my chin, and he tilted his head. His lip brushed mine, but he pulled back just enough to keep us from sinking into the kiss we both so desperately wanted.

"There's something I want you to know," he said.

"Hmm?" My lips tingled from the vibration of his voice.

His hand moved into my hair, the other drawing my body closer to his, and just before our lips touched, he whispered, "My real name is Austin."

My heart pounded, thundering his name over and over in my ears as he held me to him and kissed me. Electricity crackled through my veins and up and down my spine, and while it was far from the first time we'd touched, this kiss was charged with the thrill of a first kiss. The kind of kiss that was meant to follow hours, days, weeks of coy dancing and teasing.

The kind of kiss that meant we weren't pretending anymore.

Austin. Austin. "My real name is Austin."

Footsteps clicked on nearby pavement, but we didn't let go of each other. I wasn't worried about anyone with a badge. We weren't doing a damned thing wrong. We were lovers to anyone who happened by. Two people too caught up in the moment to take it elsewhere. Somewhere deep down, I wondered if I'd even fooled myself into believing that.

Was I fooling myself?

We broke the kiss. As he looked at me now, his eyes edged more toward gold than green this time, and he looked shy. Uncertain. Surprised. Either he was a damned good actor, or this was no longer a business transaction. And whether it was real or fake, business or pleasure, I wanted him.

"Do you..." I hesitated.

He ran his fingers through my hair. "Do I what?"

"I'm not sure where the lines are now," I whispered. "If I said I wanted to go somewhere else, I..." I gulped. "I don't know who..."

"Who do you want?" he asked. "Sabian or Austin?"

My heart pounded, and my lips tingled with the echoes of his gentle kiss. "I want..." I hesitated again, not sure if I dared cross this blurry line. "Austin."

His fingers drew an unsteady path along my cheek and the side of my neck. "You've paid to have Sabian tonight." His voice shook as badly as his fingers.

"And I think I got my money's worth." I pulled back enough to look him in the eye. "He introduced me to Austin."

"So he did." His hand curved around the back of my neck and drew me closer to him.

"Would you be opposed to going back to my place?" I asked.

Austin moistened his lips. "What about your kids?"

"They're with their father this weekend. We'll be completely alone."

"Then let's go." Even as he said it, he didn't let me go. Not yet. "But first..." He held me tighter and kissed me gently, his lips barely touching mine, but lingering a second longer than I expected. As he started to draw back, he paused. Instead of making another comment, he tilted his head and came back for another kiss.

Again our lips met softly, his pausing for a long moment before moving slowly against mine.

"I love the way you kiss," he murmured.

I gently grasped the front of his shirt. "Then kiss me again."

Chapter Eight

For a man who made his living having sex and a woman who was no stranger to casual sex or the prostitute in question, Sabian—*Austin*—and I couldn't have been more nervous or awkward when we stepped into my bedroom.

We hadn't said much on the way from the waterfront to my driveway, and now that we were in the house, we didn't speak at all. On the way up the stairs, down the hall, and into the bedroom, silence. Austin closed the door behind him, nudging it shut with his back. We both halted, looking at each other like we both hoped the other would make the first move. We were more like a couple of nervous teenagers than a pair of experienced adults.

"This is"—he muffled a cough—"not something I've done before."

"Then I guess we'll figure it out as we go."

"I guess we will."

Austin found the courage to move before I did and came across the narrow strip of distance. Eyes never leaving mine, he put his hands on the sides of my neck, and I swore I could hear his heart pounding in time with my own.

Perhaps reasoning it was a familiar—and thus safe—path toward whatever the hell we were doing, we started with the same motions we'd followed out on the waterfront. He tilted his head. I raised my chin. He leaned closer. I leaned closer. No air moved between his lips and mine, so he must have been holding his breath too. From the start, he'd always been so unafraid, the well of practiced courage when uncertainty had paralyzed me, and now he was just as unsure. God knew just what we were about to ignite, but the paper was too close to the flame to pull back now.

Our lips came together so softly I wondered if I'd imagined that first contact. Then he held me tighter and deepened the kiss. With a deeper kiss came deeper breaths, pulling in air and releasing it in sharp, cool huffs against each other's faces.

Austin broke the kiss and stroked my cheek with the backs of his fingers. "Are you sure about this?"

I couldn't have turned back now if I'd wanted to. "Are you?"

"I'm sure my boss would kill me if she knew." His hand rested on the back of my neck. "But what she doesn't know..." He kissed me again.

I held his face in both hands, my fingertips memorizing the rough texture of his stubble and the silkiness of his goatee. His jaw moved beneath my palms, a shadow of the smooth, languid movements within. The occasional thrum of a moan against my lips made my pulse soar, and the taste of his kiss and his familiar scent intoxicated me.

We both kicked off shoes and toed them out of the way. Without my heels, our height difference was more pronounced. I felt tiny in his arms, and I loved it.

Nerves made us clumsy. Hands that had steadied my hips against a hotel wall suddenly couldn't work buttons. Legs that had hooked around his waist to pull him deeper now couldn't take a step without stumbling. The mouth that could effortlessly bring shattering orgasms out of me was tentative, uncertain, moving slowly with my own.

Somehow, though buttons baffled me just then, I got his jacket unbuttoned and off his shoulders. With a shrug, he dropped it behind him, and seconds later, his vest landed on top of it, followed by his tie in a flutter of shiny crimson silk. We both struggled to unbutton his shirt and finally gave up, pushing it over his head instead.

He unzipped the back of my dress and slid it off my shoulders. When it was gone, pooling forgotten at our feet, he bent to kiss my neck, wrapping his warm arms around me once again. Fingertips moved against my back, and a second later, my bra went slack. I let it tumble down my arms. It caught on my hand, and I shook it away, silently cursing at it like it was a spiderweb that wouldn't let go. When it finally fell away, he drew me back to him, and the heat of his skin drew the breath right out of my lungs.

Then he kissed me and nudged me toward the bed. Legs shaking beneath me, I moved with no conscious thought, responding to his steps like a dancer being led. His kiss made my head spin, anticipation made my heart race, and with every inch of ground we gained across the floor, my knees weakened. Had we needed just one more step, I was certain I would have collapsed, but when we reached the bed, it was Austin—not gravity, not my own liquefied limbs—who gently laid me down.

He took my hands and pinned them to the pillow beside my head, his forearms over mine and our fingers laced together. Then he kissed me. God in heaven, did he kiss me.

Sabian hadn't been a forceful kisser since day one, and Austin didn't start now. Gentle and sensual. Tasting, not devouring. One minute, his tongue explored my mouth. The next, he was content just to let his lips move against mine. Always changing, always different from one moment to another, always perfect.

He broke the kiss and started to pull away, but I lifted my head off the pillow to follow him, seeking more and finding it when he returned to me and kissed me like that again. After a moment, he tried and failed to break away again. He tightened his grasp on my hands and pressed his hips against me, his rock-hard erection making me whimper with anticipation.

He released one of my hands and let his own drift down my arm, my side, the curve of my waist. When he got to the thin garter on my thigh, he groaned softly into my kiss. Curling his fingertips against my skin, he encouraged me to hook my leg around his waist. I did, and he slid his hand over my hip and traced the strap up my thigh.

"You wore a garter again," he breathed. "Fuck..."

"You like it?"

"Damn right I do. But I like you even better with nothing on." He unclipped the garter straps and slowly pushed my stocking down my leg. When it was off, he did the same to the other leg. I ran my bare foot up the back of his leg, the soft fabric of his pants against my bare skin making me shiver.

I reached between us, and when I gently squeezed him through his slacks, he groaned and broke the kiss, letting his head fall beside mine.

He shifted onto one arm, reaching between us with the other. I thought he'd push my hand away, but instead, he unbuckled his belt. Then and only then did he nudge my hand out of the way, but only long enough to unzip his slacks. We both pushed them over his hips, and when they were far enough out of the way, he guided my hand back to his hard cock.

"Feel what you do to me?" he murmured. "Fuck, I want you so bad, Jocelyn."

"Oh, it's mutual."

"Is it, now?" He grinned and slid his hand between my thighs. "So your pussy must be—" He paused when his fingers found what they sought. "Oh, God, baby, you are so fucking wet." He teased with only his fingertips, drawing moan after moan of frustration out of me as he kept his magic fingers from sliding deep enough to find my G-spot.

"Austin...you're..." *Fuck me, damn it. Please.*

His fingers moved to my clit, and there they drew slow, lazy circles that sent sparks crackling up the length of my spine. He barely touched me, but it was intense. Breathtaking. So good it hurt.

I bit my lip and closed my eyes, trying to will myself to speak over the cacophony of pleasure-bordering-on-pain that bombarded my senses, to tell him how much I loved what he did and how much I wanted him to fuck me, but words failed me.

"All the way here," he whispered, his lips barely leaving mine as his fingers slowly slipped a little deeper into my pussy, "I was thinking about all the things I wanted to do to you." Deeper. "And now that we're here…" Almost to the perfect spot. "I don't even know where to start." His lips met mine in the same moment his palm came to rest over my clit.

"Oh, God," I whispered when he broke the kiss. "I… Please…"

"I could go down on you and make you come a few times," he said. "Or I could keep doing this until you beg me to fuck you." He pressed harder with this hand, destroying any chance I had of speaking. "But I can't stop thinking," he went on, beckoning against my G-spot as he spoke, "about the fact that you're so wet I could fuck you *right now.*"

"*Yes.*" One word burst out of me, the best I could do in my current state.

I opened my eyes, and we held each other's gazes. He parted his lips as if he was about to speak, paused as if he couldn't find the words, and kissed me instead. He slowly withdrew his fingers, and together, without breaking this long, delicious kiss, we sat up.

"I think I still have too many clothes on," he murmured against my lips.

"We should take care of that, then." My heart pounded. Anticipation? Nerves? Terrified of and dying for our first time that wasn't really our first time?

Whatever the case, there was no turning back now, and with all the clumsy grace of first-time lovers, we got out of the rest of our clothes. Before he dropped his slacks off the side of the bed, he pulled a condom out of his pocket. When he reached for the nightstand to set it aside, I grabbed his wrist.

"No." I licked my lips. "Put it on. Now."

A grin teased the corners of his mouth. "You don't want me to—"

"Please, Austin." My God, just the taste of his real name on my lips turned me on beyond words.

He tore the wrapper with his teeth and, with hands that I'd never before seen so unsteady, rolled on the condom. Then I was in his arms again. Had his kiss always made me this light-headed? I didn't know. I didn't care, because it certainly made me this light-headed *now*.

Every bit of my attention was focused solely on the sexy, sensual way his mouth moved with mine, but just beyond the edges of my awareness, I knew we were moving. Shifting. Entangling. When he broke the kiss, he was over me, his arms beneath my back and his hips settling between my parted thighs. I took a breath, a shiver of anticipation rushing through me.

He bent to kiss me, our lips meeting for the briefest second only to part in a simultaneous exhale when he slipped inside me. He moved slowly, and I rolled my hips with him, our eyes locked on each other. The expression in his reflected the overwhelmed feeling in me, and the breathtaking sensations surging through me went above and beyond anything that was bought and paid for.

There was something unnerving about it, something thrilling but terrifying, as if something changed between us with each stroke, with each brush of his fingertips against my face. He closed his eyes and kissed me, and I was lost in him, lost in the intimacy I hadn't expected this evening.

He rested on his forearms, his fingertips caressing my face as mine combed through his hair. Even as his hips moved faster, as he electrified every nerve inside me, it was his kiss that held my full attention. My body ached for release, but I was afraid to encourage him to move any faster, because he might break this kiss.

After an eternity—but not nearly long enough— he did just that, raising his head and looking into my eyes. He touched my face, and he took a breath as if to speak, but a shiver cut him off, so he just kissed me again. His hand slid around to the back of my neck, then up into my hair, cradling my head as he parted my lips with his tongue.

As our kiss deepened, my arms tightened around him. Our bodies slowed, still moving together but with every stroke losing what little speed we'd gained. Before long, only our mouths moved. He was inside me, deep inside me, but we were both still, just tasting and breathing each other. Every place we made contact— skin on skin, lips on lips, even his breath whispering across my cheek whenever he exhaled through his nose—was electrified, pulsing with intensity.

His lips never leaving mine, he withdrew slowly, then pushed back in. He picked up speed again, but still he kissed me, and I held on tight, determined not to lose contact with his incredible mouth. The soft movements of his lips and tongue were punctuated by sharp rhythmic breaths that came in time with his quickening strokes, but even the occasional gasp or moan only separated our lips for a heartbeat.

I dug my fingernails into his back just enough for him to feel it. Then I raked them down either side of his spine, shivering at the ragged breath that escaped his throat.

"Baby, you feel so good," he moaned, arching his back against my nails. "Fuck, I..."

I rocked my hips back, pulling him deeper, meeting him thrust for deep, violent thrust.

"Oh, my God," he breathed. Through clenched teeth, he said, "You want it harder, don't you?" He didn't wait for me respond. He pushed himself up and fucked me *hard*. His arms and shoulders rippled beneath sweat-glazed skin with every move he made, and the sight of his muscles and tattoos alone nearly sent me over the edge.

"Austin, I'm..." I gasped for breath. "Don't stop... Please, don't stop."

"I won't. Not until you come." His rhythm faltered when he met my eyes. Recovering quickly, he held my gaze, and his eyes were on fire with lust, with need. "You're close, aren't you? I can feel it, you're..."

Looking right back into his eyes, I whispered the one word my tongue could form: "*Faster.*"

Sliding his hands under my back, he gripped my shoulders and let his head fall next to mine, fucking me hard enough to knock the air out of me. In seconds he pushed me over the edge, and everything went white, and just like the last time—just like almost every damned time he made me come—I tried to cry out but couldn't. My voice stopped somewhere in my throat, and only a soft moan, barely more than a sigh, left my lips. The faint sound echoed in what little silence wasn't already consumed by the bedsprings and headboard and our bodies colliding with every thrust. It wasn't nearly enough to do justice to the wildfire of intensity he unleashed inside me, but it was all I could manage.

Austin moaned. "Jesus, Jocelyn, you're so—"

Our eyes met, and his rhythm faltered. Though he recovered quickly, neither of us looked away, and the electricity thrumming in the air wasn't just because of the way our bodies moved together. The longer we looked at each other, the slower we moved—or perhaps it was time that slowed down, I couldn't be sure—but still the intensity grew as our eyes made a kind of unspoken connection, exchanging a level of intimacy that thrilled and terrified me. We weren't supposed to be this close, but I'd be damned if I was going to pull away.

"Oh my God," I heard myself say. The sound of my voice seemed to shake us both out of paralysis. He came down to me and kissed me as he fucked me hard and fast. I wrapped my arms around him and—perhaps in spite of my better judgment—surrendered.

Whether we intended it, or wanted it, or even thought it was a good idea, this wasn't what I'd paid for. Tonight we'd slipped beyond the realms of escort and client and into a comfortable intimacy two strangers couldn't possibly share, and now that intimacy carried into this moment as we blurred the line between fucking and making love.

No—as we *crossed* that line.

It was much too soon to know *what* was happening between us, but much too late to deny that it was. This wasn't business anymore.

"My God, Jocelyn, I could do this all night," he groaned. "All goddamned night. You feel so—" He cut himself off with a sharp breath, closing his eyes and slowing down, taking a few long, deep breaths until he was back in control. Then he looked into my eyes and picked up speed again. "Your body is...perfect." He slowed again, his body shaking from either exertion or his struggle to stay in control. Maybe both.

He was close, and yet he held back, but I wanted his orgasm like I'd wanted my own. The very thought of watching him come, feeling it, made me bite my lip to hold back a whimper. Running my fingers through his sweaty hair, I said, "I want you to come, Austin."

As soon as I whispered his name, his breath caught, and he forced himself as deep inside me as he could. His fingers tightened over my shoulders, hot breath rushed past my neck, and for the first time since I'd known him, he truly let go, a throaty groan escaping his lips as his body shuddered against mine.

After the shaking subsided, he raised his head and looked into my eyes again. As soon as our eyes met, I knew I was right about the intimacy between us. His expression mirrored my exhilarating fear that we'd crossed some unseen line between physical desire and emotional need.

While he got up to get rid of the condom, my stomach fluttered. Tense, queasy nervousness replaced the lingering shudders of my orgasm. Without the distraction of the need for release, I couldn't keep the unsettling questions about this and about us away from the forefront of my mind.

His return didn't help. He lay beside me, and when he looked in my eyes, the same questions were undeniably in his.

I took a breath. "Well, this was…unexpected."

"You're telling me." He brushed a strand of unruly hair out of my face. "So, what do we do now?"

"No idea."

Austin pursed his lips. Then he cleared his throat. "Whether it was a good idea or not, I have to admit I liked it."

"So did I." Did I ever.

"Would it be too forward or awkward for me to say I'd like to do it again?"

I swallowed. "Probably. But I would too. So, whether we should or not…" I raised my eyebrows. "Sounds like we both want to."

"Yeah, it does." His touched my face. "Why don't we just start out simple? No strings attached, no expectations. Maybe just a date that doesn't start with you having your credit card preapproved."

I laughed. "That would be a good start, wouldn't it?"

Austin chuckled. "A good start, yes." His expression turned more serious. "So with that in mind, do you have plans tomorrow night?"

"Not at the moment, no."

"Why don't we start with dinner and go from there?"

"Sounds like a plan."

Chapter Nine

Since his apartment was about halfway between my house and the restaurant we'd chosen, we agreed that I'd meet him at his place and he'd drive. We were headed for a low-key café tonight, a world apart from last night's five-star. I was dressed casually, but I couldn't say I felt terribly relaxed. Part of me was still puzzled about what we were doing and how we'd gotten to this point.

I was probably more nervous tonight than I'd been the first night. Before, we'd bypassed all the bullshit that usually preceded a one-night stand. We'd skipped the games, passed Go, he'd collected a few hundred dollars, and now we had to somehow start from the beginning. This wasn't the first time we'd met, wouldn't be the first time we'd slept together if we did, but it *was* the first time we'd started out without the pretense of a prearranged, paid deal.

I wasn't opposed to that, or I wouldn't have come to his apartment, but I had to admit I didn't have the faintest idea what we were doing or how to do it.

Only one way to find out, I reasoned as I pulled into the parking lot.

The Austin who answered the door was a far cry from the Sabian who'd walked into the restaurant last night. I'd never seen him dressed down before, and he still looked like pure sex in jeans and a half-buttoned black shirt over a white T-shirt.

"You're right on time." He kissed my cheek, then stood back to let me in.

"I'm kind of obsessive about that," I said. "Being early or on time."

"So am I." He nodded down the hall. "I just need to get my jacket and wallet. Come on in." I followed him down the hall into his living room, and he made a sweeping gesture at his surroundings. "This is my place. Isn't exactly the Playboy Mansion, but it does the job."

"Seems like a nice place to me." It was a small apartment, probably a two-bedroom. In the living room, one wall had been painted a deep red as an accent wall, which complemented the simple black-and-white furniture.

Beneath his flat-screen TV, a couple of game consoles caught my eye.

"Looks like you and my son would get along great," I said.

He looked up from getting a jacket out of the hall closet. "Oh?"

"Xbox. He and his father love it."

"It's a bit of a bad habit of mine. I probably play it more than I should." Austin pulled his jacket on. "Then again, it helps with manual dexterity, so..." Our eyes met, and he winked.

I laughed. "I can't complain about it, then, can I?"

"I should hope not. Well, if you're ready, I think—" His brow furrowed and his eyes lost focus while he searched his pockets. "Damn it, what did I..."

"What's wrong?"

He clicked his tongue. "Wallet. I'm always leaving that thing all over the house. I'll be right back." He disappeared into the bedroom, and I took in more of the scenery.

The walls, red and white alike, were lined with colorful framed photographs of varying sizes. They were mostly landscapes and cityscapes with the odd still life and a flower arrangement that was anything but bland.

"You don't put your own work on display?" I asked when he came back into the room.

"Sure I do." He smiled. "Everything you see on the walls is my work."

"It is? But I thought you were a paint—" The hand-painted signature, *A. Landis*, on the bottom right corner of a photo of a waterfall caught my eye. When I looked closer, I noticed a faint imperfection in the riverbank. Not a mistake per se, just a division between light and dark where a photograph would have been slightly sharper. Looking at the whole picture again, I realized it wasn't a photograph at all.

"These are...paintings?"

He nodded, lips pulling into a shy smile. "Well, that one is. Those two are mostly colored pencil." He indicated an image of Times Square and another of a cathedral. Like the waterfall, they were photos at first glance, hand-rendered at second.

"Austin, these are amazing."

He gave a quiet laugh and dropped his gaze, cheeks coloring.

"I'm serious. These are..." I shook my head. His work as was close to photorealism as I'd ever seen. "These are incredible. I can't believe you have a hard time selling this stuff."

"Well, it would probably help if I put more effort into selling it," he said. "I'm admittedly not the best salesman in the world, particularly when it's my own work." He shot me a boyish grin. "Whoring myself isn't my strong point."

I eyed him. "Now isn't that ironic?"

"Just a little." He grinned. "Honestly, if I had someone like the girls running the agency putting my artwork out there, I might have better luck. I'm just not a salesman."

"You may not be a salesman, but you're definitely an artist. I'm amazed at these. I really am."

His grin turned back into to a shy smile. "Thanks."

"My son wants to learn to—" I stopped, rolling my eyes. "Sorry."

Austin cocked his head. "What about?"

"I don't like being 'that mom' who talks about her kids constantly, but..." I shrugged. "They are a big part of my life. So they come up a lot."

"I wouldn't expect any less." He cupped my chin and kissed me gently. "It's okay. You can talk about your kids."

"Okay. But promise me one thing."

He raised his eyebrows.

"If I start rambling incessantly about them, promise me you'll tell me to shut up."

He laughed. "I don't think that'll be a problem. So, your son wants to learn...?"

"He loves drawing, and he really, really wants to learn to do it well." I gestured at one of Austin's paintings. "Like, *that* well."

Austin opened his mouth to speak but hesitated. After a second, he said, "Well, I'd offer to give him some pointers, but..."

"Oh. Right." I shifted my weight. "Maybe someday."

Our eyes met, and something in my gut twisted. Shit, second time in his presence as something other than his client, and I was using words like 'someday'? *Slow down, Jocelyn. Slow down.*

But Austin just smiled. "Maybe someday." Then he quickly cleared his throat. "So, should we get out of here?"

"Lead the way."

Down in the parking lot, Austin opened the car door for me before he went around to the driver's side. For whatever reason, I'd had this illusion that men in his line of work had candy-apple red convertible sports cars parked in front of their penthouse lofts. Short of a hippie-painted VW Bug, Austin's car couldn't have been any further from what I'd imagined: at the foot of a modest apartment building, a nondescript maroon four-door. It was probably a few years old, undoubtedly had plenty of miles on the odometer, but it was immaculate inside and out. I guessed Austin was the kind of guy who could make a car last to two hundred thousand before it fell apart.

He turned the key in the ignition, and as the engine came to life, the radio kicked on in the middle of a Garth Brooks song. Austin quickly clicked it off.

"You listen to country?" I asked. Another stereotype shot down, apparently.

"Among other things." He put the car in reverse and backed out of the space. "What do you listen to?"

"Whatever's on the radio that isn't rap, a commercial, or a political commentary."

Shifting into drive, he chuckled. "Yeah, me too. I usually just channel-surf, but I have a few presets. Country, classic rock, one of the news stations that actually does regular traffic reports when it's supposed to."

"I'm about the same way," I said. "Do you listen to that new country station?"

"Which one—106?"

"No, the other one. It's 97.3, isn't it?"

He wrinkled his nose. "Can't stand it. The deejays are so..."

"Obnoxious?"

"Yes, that. Especially the morning show."

"Oh, I know. I can't listen to them for more than a few minutes."

"Neither can I." He slowed to a stop at a red light. "The late-night deejay is pretty good, though."

"I've only heard him a time or two. I'm not usually listening to the radio at that hour."

"I'm usually on my way home at some point during his show."

Austin glanced at me, and we both quickly looked out the windshield. These occasional reminders of his job would probably take some getting used to.

To lighten the mood, I said, "I never thought of country music as a chaser for that kind of thing."

He laughed. "Keeps me awake until I get home."

"That's a plus, isn't it?"

"Yeah, it definitely is." The light turned green, and as he pulled across the intersection, he said, "I've also been known to listen to rap if it's really late and I'm starting to fall asleep."

"I suppose that could help," I said. "It would probably just make me drive faster so I got home and didn't have to listen to it anymore."

"That's not too far from the truth," he said, chuckling. "It's actually pretty good for keeping me awake. Don't know if it's the bass, the beat, or the fact that it annoys the hell out of me, but it does the job."

About fifteen minutes after we left his apartment, Austin pulled up in front of the restaurant to let me out. While I went in to get us a table, he went to find a parking space.

The café was more crowded than we'd anticipated, so there was a bit of a wait. No more than about ten minutes, the hostess promised, so I put our names on the list. When he arrived, Austin stood behind me and wrapped his arms around my waist, kissing my cheek gently. I put my hands over his and—completely defying everything I'd ever done with men in the past—simply let myself be held. And I loved it. I adored physical affection, but it usually took me a while to settle into it with a new guy. It was unusual for me, this casual affection with someone new. In the past, it was months before someone could rest a hand on me without startling me or making me wonder what to do with my own hands.

Then again, we were hardly in a position to be uncomfortable touching each other, so I tried to just enjoy it and not read too much into it.

Still, I had to admit how oddly relaxed things were between us was compared to a normal first date. Of course it wasn't our first time breathing the same air, but it was the first time we'd met without any pretenses of this being a business transaction. No money was being exchanged this time. We'd already had sex. Repeatedly. There was no need to impress each other, to woo each other into bed. It was a safe bet we'd end up there tonight. For now, we could let our hair down and just enjoy food and conversation. And, apparently, gentle affection.

After we'd been seated and placed our orders, Austin folded his hands on the table and looked at me. "So, you said your son has an artistic side. What about your daughter?"

I sipped my water and set the glass down. "You sure you want to get me started on my kids? I can go on about them all night."

He smiled. "They're part of your life, and I want to know about you. So yes."

"Don't say I didn't warn you." I rested my forearms on the table. "I think Lex is going to be my science buff. That kid soaks up information like a sponge. Taught herself to read when she was three, and she loves anything science related."

"And she's how old?"

"Coming on eight," I said. "But take her out on a clear night, and she can point out constellations I've never even heard of."

"Sounds like a kid who'd use the hell out of a telescope."

"You're not wrong there. We're waiting until she's a little bit older, but Michael and I have been talking about getting her one." I played with the coaster under my water glass. "I know, I know, every parent talks like their kid is the cutest, smartest, fastest, whatever, but seriously, this kid catches me off guard sometimes."

"Really?"

"Oh God, yes. She's got her dad's dry sense of humor and can deadpan and bullshit like nobody's business."

"How so?"

"Like, a couple of weekends ago, we were sitting there eating breakfast," I said. "It was absolutely pouring down rain. Freezing cold, windy as hell, nastiest weather in ages. She looks out the window and says with a totally straight face, 'Mom, this looks like a good day to go to the beach.'"

Austin laughed. "She must keep you on your toes."

"You have no idea. And it doesn't help that her preferred form of entertainment, if you can get her in front of a television, is British comedy."

His eyebrows jumped. "Seriously?"

I nodded. "Her dad's had her watching *Blackadder* and *Red Dwarf* since she was an infant. She'd rather watch those than cartoons."

"And she *gets* them?" he said. "I mean, at her age, she gets the humor?"

"More of it than you'd think." I laughed and absently brushed a strand of hair out of my face. "Fortunately, her dad is conservative enough he doesn't explain some of the racier jokes to her, figuring when she's old enough to get it, she'll get it."

"Smart man," Austin said with a quiet laugh. "Speaking of your ex, if you don't mind my asking, how do the kids deal with you two being divorced?"

"It's not as bad as I thought it would be, honestly," I said. "Mikey took a while to adjust, but Lex was so young she doesn't even remember us being married."

"And the two of you get along?"

I nodded. "Oh yes. In fact, our custody arrangement is kind of nice. Michael and I each get a break to collect and regroup a bit for a week; then we can devote ourselves fully when we have the kids. It's not ideal, but it works, the kids are well-adjusted, and all the adults get along."

"Can't ask for much more than that," he said. "I've always wondered how kids deal with it. Having their parents split, I mean."

"Yours are still married, I take it?"

"Thirty-seven years and counting."

Well, there went another stereotype. So much for the idea that a sex worker must have come from a broken home and a miserable childhood.

He went on, "Hell, when I was a kid, I used to panic whenever they'd fight. All they had to do was raise their voices, and I started worrying they'd break up."

"Really?"

He nodded, rolling his eyes. "Yeah, it was stupid. My parents were happily married then and still are now. I was just so afraid of ending up with divorced parents like most of my friends."

"I don't think it's stupid at all," I said. "My folks broke up when I was a teenager, so I really didn't want to do it to my kids, but..." I trailed off, shrugging.

Austin smiled. "Divorced or not, it sounds like you've done better by your kids than some married parents do."

"We do the best we can."

Throughout dinner, the conversation wandered. Families, past relationships, work, the usual date material. The odd mention of his occupation jarred me, reminding me of the reality that this was the man I'd recently paid for sex. More than once. Knowing what I did about him, though, it didn't bother me like I thought it should. Like it would have in another lifetime.

There was a time when it would have been easy to make assumptions and paint his entire existence with the brush of being a male escort, but it was different now. I'd seen his artwork, his everyday car parked in front of his everyday apartment, and the way he blushed and dropped his gaze when I complimented his work. In his past, there were college years, a rocky marriage, and a three-week cross-country road trip with some friends after high school. He talked about his nieces and nephews the way I talked about my kids. Going to bed with a complete stranger in exchange for a few hundred dollars he could do, but there wasn't enough money in the world to get him past his fear of public speaking.

More and more, he was simply Austin. What he did and how we met became less and less material. In the back of my mind, I wondered if this, whatever it was, could go anywhere. I wondered if it *should*. After all, if it did, there would come a time when he'd have to meet my kids, and I owed it to my ex-husband to be honest with him about who I was dating. In theory, Austin and I could keep Sabian a secret, but if Michael ever found out? If he figured out I'd been bringing a prostitute around his children? That could get ugly.

But I was getting ahead of myself. This was just dinner. A date. Some food, some conversation, and probably another night between the sheets.

Sitting back with a cup of coffee in his hand, Austin glanced at his watch. "It's still pretty early. Would you be interested in catching a movie after we're done here?"

"I have to admit, I'm not a fan of movies on dates."

"Is that right?"

I nodded. "Well, a first date at least. I usually prefer to wait until I've been seeing someone long enough that I don't feel like I'm sitting in silence in the dark with a total stranger that I should be getting to know."

Austin laughed. "I know exactly what you mean. Though there is something to be said for getting to know a stranger in a theater with stadium seating and armrests that can be lifted up and out of the way." He winked.

"Are you suggesting you'd use a movie theater for something it wasn't intended for?"

He snorted. "Please. A dark room like that is meant for one thing, and one thing only."

"Watching movies, last I checked."

He shrugged. "That or a blowjob."

I laughed. "I can't say I've ever done that in a theater."

"Really?" He grinned and reached across the table to lay his hand over mine. "Maybe we'll have to change that."

"Maybe we will." I turned my hand over under his and ran my thumb back and forth across his wrist. "For now, you'll just have to put up with conversation."

"Oh, fine. If you insist." He clicked his tongue and rolled his eyes.

"But if you're good, maybe we can go to a movie later."

He trailed his fingertips along the underside of my forearm. "Or maybe we could just skip the movie."

"Well, what fun is that?"

He grinned. "I can see we're going to get along very well."

The waitress appeared just then and laid the check on the table in a black leather folder. Austin and I both reached for it, his hand landing on top of mine.

"I've got this," he said.

"I can pay. It's no problem."

"You paid last night."

"It was just a bottle of wine."

"That bottle of wine was expensive." He grinned. "And so was I."

I shivered. "Yes, but you were well worth it."

"Well, when I'm off the clock, I'm a gentleman. I'm not making a lady pay."

I laughed. "So you're not a gentleman when you're on the clock?"

"Of course I am," he said. "I'm just not expected or allowed to foot the bill."

"Why don't we go Dutch this time?"

Hand still over mine, Austin leaned toward me and lowered his voice. "To be completely serious, you're the first woman in I don't know how long who's sat through a date with me, knowing full well what I do for a living, and treated me like a human being." His other hand slid under mine and pulled the check free. "I don't want that to cost you a dime."

I swallowed, watching him pull his bank card out and slip it into the folder.

"Okay," I said quietly, "but the next one's on me."

He winked. "We'll see about that."

The waitress came and took the check. A moment later, she returned. Austin signed the receipt, and we put on our coats. As we headed out the door, he laced his fingers between mine, and we exchanged smiles.

Outside in the crisp evening air, he said, "So where do you want to go?"

I could think of at least one place. I cleared my throat. "Oh, I don't know. We could just walk and see if anything looks interesting."

"We can do that."

I couldn't say which of us picked a direction or if we just started walking without thinking, but hand in hand we strolled down the sidewalk. We made light conversation for a while before Austin stopped in front of a store window. I thought something had caught his eye, but instead of checking out the display, he looked at me.

"I wasn't kidding about what I said in the restaurant," he said, running his thumb back and forth across my hand. "This is the first time I've had anything like a real, normal date in a long time."

"Their loss," I whispered. "There's obviously a lot more to you than your job, so..."

There it was again, that shy smile and the dropped gaze. "Yeah, there is, but you're..." He trailed off, swallowing hard. "You're the first one who's seen that. So thank you."

I smiled. "You're welcome."

We held each other's gazes for a moment. Then he gave a quiet laugh and looked at the display beside us, then the pavement, then somewhere else. Finally, he looked down at our hands.

"This is so...weird."

"Which part?"

"The part where I...do what I do for a living, but I..." He looked at me through his lashes. "But now, with you, I feel like a clueless school kid again."

I moistened my lips. "What do you mean?"

"Like, I'm scared of screwing something up."

"I don't think you have much to worry about," I said. "I'm as clueless as you are right now."

He smiled and touched my face. "Then I guess we'll just stumble through it and hope for the best."

"I can handle that."

His thumb made gentle, uneven arcs across my cheekbone. Barely whispering, he said, "What I do know is that right now, I really, really want to kiss you."

I swallowed hard. "Then kiss me."

Chapter Ten

Austin kicked his apartment door shut behind us, and we stumbled down the hall. I shoved his jacket off his shoulders, and as soon as his hands were free from the sleeves, he tried to unbutton my blouse, but he only made it to the second button before he tangled his fingers in my hair instead. I went for his belt, but somehow my hands ended up on his chest, grasping handfuls of his shirt and pulling him down the hall toward his bedroom. Someone stumbled. We tried to right ourselves, stumbled again.

Austin grunted when I forced him up against the wall, but he didn't break the kiss. We were both breathless and desperate, and with this kind of feverish, horny kiss, there was no leaving this place, not even to make the journey down the short hallway to his bedroom. My need had reached a breaking point, and something had to give. Right here. Right now.

I started on his shirt, struggling with the buttons. Too many. Too goddamned many buttons. Shaking hands, eyes that wouldn't focus.

Too many buttons, but only one buckle.

His spine straightened when I went for his belt.

"Bedroom," he whispered, panting against my lips. He tried to guide me back, but I put a hand on his shoulder and kept him still.

"No," I said. "Here."

"But I, we—" He closed his eyes and let his head fall back against the wall when I drew his zipper down. "Oh, Jesus..."

"Right here. I can't wait." I didn't give him a chance to protest or even comprehend before I went to my knees.

"Oh fuck," he whispered when I circled the head of his cock with my tongue. "That's...oh God..." His hand hit the wall beside him. The other gently grasped my hair, fingers trembling against my scalp.

I didn't think it was possible for me to be more turned on than this, but the heat and salt of his skin were arousing beyond belief. Nearly deep-throating him, I moaned softly, shivering when he gasped.

I looked up at him, and my skin prickled with goose bumps. He was the very picture of arousal: rumpled shirt, furrowed brow, parted lips. I went down on him with renewed fervor, trembling each time he gasped or his fingers twitched in my hair. His hand couldn't decide whether to grasp or stroke; his knees couldn't decide whether to lock or buckle.

I squeezed a little harder with my fingers as my lips followed my hand almost all the way to the base of his cock. The pulsing against my tongue and palm told me he was close, but it was the long, breathless moan that told me just how close. He whispered something, his lips forming words that didn't quite make it to my ears.

Then he said, "Wait. Stop, baby; I don't want to come yet."

I rocked back on my heels, looking up at him while I still stroked his cock. He gently grasped my wrist to stop my hand.

"Stand up," he said, panting. "Stand up, so we...so..." He swallowed, nodding down the hall toward the bedroom. I rose on shaking legs, and the second I was upright, his arms were around me again.

We made it precisely one step closer to the bedroom.

Austin's forehead touched mine, and his breath came in short, sharp gasps. "I can't wait. I want to fuck you." His palpable desperation almost knocked my already precarious knees out from under me. I moistened my lips. Before I could speak, he whispered, "I want you, Jocelyn. Please. Now."

"But we—"

"Please, baby." He licked his lips then whispered, "Right. Here." Our eyes met, and we both caught our breath.

Forget the bedroom.

I grabbed the front of his shirt and dragged him down to the floor with me. We tried to tear off clothes, then settled for just getting them out of the way. He fished a couple of condoms out of his back pocket and dropped them where they'd be within easy reach.

Without a word, he sat up while I slipped my panties off. He pushed his jeans just past his hips before coming back down to me, kissing me passionately. Between the two of us, we got the condom unwrapped and on him. Once it was *finally* on, he pushed my skirt up to my hips, and I wrapped my legs around his waist.

With one quick thrust, his cock was all the way inside me, the sudden intensity bringing tears to my eyes. We both froze, neither breathing, neither moving.

After a moment, I whimpered. "Oh God."

"Oh, fuck, baby..." He sounded almost in pain and shivered, letting his head fall beside mine as he withdrew slowly. "You've got me so fucking turned on, there's"—he pushed back in, a sharp, cool breath brushing past my neck—"there's no way I'm going to last like this."

"I don't care," I said between gasping for breath. "Oh, my God, you feel amazing." I raked my nails down the back of his shirt, and he released a sharp hiss of breath. Abruptly, he pushed himself upright, out of my reach.

Icy panic swept through me. Thinking I'd hurt him, I quickly said, "Sorry, I—" But I stopped when he pulled his shirt off and tossed it aside before coming back down to me.

"Don't apologize." Kissing me breathlessly, he slid his hands under my back and hooked his fingers over my shoulders. "I just had to get that out of your way." He gasped when my nails raked across his shoulders. Once again, I thought I'd hurt him, but he groaned into my kiss and arched his back, pushing against my nails and driving himself deep inside me.

"Oh, fuck," I breathed. "That feels incredible."

He thrust faster now, every stroke sending me further into oblivion. The sharp, metallic sound of his belt buckle marked time as he found that perfect rhythm between *can't get enough* and *can't take any more.*

"Oh my God, oh fuck, Austin…" I couldn't even remember that I wanted to drag my nails across his skin, because all I could do now was hold on to him. With nails, with fingers, with arms that didn't even feel like my own anymore.

I rocked my hips in time with his thrusts, pulling him deeper. The first pulses of an orgasm rippled up my spine, and a violent shudder drove him deeper still, sending waves of hot ice from my G-spot to every nerve in my body.

"Look at me," he said. I was almost afraid to. If the intensity in his eyes matched what I felt, I was sure my heart would forget how to beat. "Look at me, Jocelyn," he pleaded, his voice trembling. Taking a breath, I opened my eyes. The intensity was there, all that and more, but my heart still beat—faster now, thundering in my ears—and I held his gaze as if it was the one thing left on this plane of existence that I *could* hold on to.

"Oh God, I'm gonna come," I moaned.

"So am I," he said through clenched teeth. A gasp, then a shiver. He groaned, almost whimpered, and the sheer delirious lust in his voice was more than I could take. My entire body seized, and I clawed his back as everything in and around me exploded.

"Fuck, I'm so close, but I—" He gasped, picking up speed once more. "I just don't want…to fucking…*stop…*"

Three times he slowed down and regained control, but the fourth time—whether by choice or defeat—he surrendered. His lips parted as if he wanted to cry out but couldn't, and with one last thrust, he shuddered, whispered my name, and came.

When the dust settled, we didn't move. We breathed in unison, the exact same rapid, irregular breaths, and I wondered if I would have forgotten how to breathe altogether without him there to remind me. We were a tangled mess of shaking limbs and disheveled clothing, holding on to each other for dear life in the middle of his hallway, kissing between gasps. I was vaguely aware of the mild sting in my back and shoulder blades from grinding against the carpet, but it didn't bother me. I'd just had some of the hottest sex of my life, and a little collateral damage was a small price to pay for it.

Austin put his weight on his forearm and pushed himself up. "That," he whispered, grimacing as he pulled out, "was unbelievable."

"You're telling me."

Somehow we got to our feet and into the bedroom. Austin got rid of the condom, and we both shed the last of our clothes before sinking into bed together. We held each other close, kissing lazily, and I had no doubt tonight was far from over. The air between us was still charged with need. Though it simmered beneath the surface now, the intense hunger tempered for the time being by a couple of orgasms, we weren't done yet.

After a while, he looked at me, running his fingers through my hair. "So, can I talk you into staying here tonight?"

"Depends on what's in it for me."

"Oh, does it?" He laughed. "Well, in that case, I'll have to make it worth your while, won't I?"

"Yes, you will."

"Hmm." He cupped my breast and drew circles around my nipple with his thumb. "I could promise you a home-cooked breakfast in the morning."

"Ooh, tempting."

"Or, failing that, I have more compelling arguments if you're particularly stubborn."

I raised an eyebrow, trying not to grin. "In that case, I'm going to be particularly stubborn."

Austin ran the tip of his tongue along his lower lip. "Are you, now? Well..." He pinched my nipple between his thumb and forefinger, pressing just hard enough to bring an involuntary moan of pleasure to my lips. "Like that?"

"Mm-hmm."

Still teasing my nipple, he kissed me gently. "I thought so. And now that I have your attention..." His hand left my breast and drifted down my side. "I was thinking that if you're going to be particularly stubborn, I'll just have to do things like promise to keep you awake until well past any reasonable hour." He dipped his head and kissed my neck while his hand gently parted my thighs. "And maybe keep my neighbors awake in the process."

I shivered, and not just because his fingers had begun a slow, spiraling path toward my clit. "Is that—" His fingers inched closer to my clit, making it almost impossible to speak. I licked my lips. "Is that so?"

Closer. "But just in case you're not duly convinced it's worth your while to stay here..." Closer. "I should also let you know I have every intention of making sure you can't walk in the morning."

"I think..." God, his fingers were *so close*. "I think if you put it like that, I might just have to stay and see if you'll follow through."

He raised his head and looked me in the eye. His fingers were dangerously close now, but just circled, neither closing in nor backing away. "Do you doubt my sincerity or my ability?"

"I don't doubt either," I said. "I just want you to do it."

"So you'll stay, then?"

Before I could respond, his fingertips brushed over my clit, and lightning erupted behind my eyelids and along the length of my spine.

"You still haven't answered my question, Jocelyn." His fingers reversed direction, igniting fresh lightning. "Do you want to stay tonight, or should I let you go?"

I grabbed the back of his neck and pulled him down to kiss me.

He got the message.

Chapter Eleven

I slowly swam out of the darkness of sleep and into the darkness of the night. In spite of the heavy shadows shrouding everything into an abstract black blur, I blinked, trying to focus my eyes anyway, taking one of my mind's habitual steps toward a coherent state.

Austin's chest was against my back, his arm over my waist. His breath whispered across the back of my neck, and I realized he'd shifted in his sleep, nudging me just enough to wake me up. I smiled to myself. I could certainly think of worse reasons to be disturbed. Fidgeting just slightly, I changed my position enough to ease a vague ache in my hip, and when I did, his fingers twitched against my skin.

His breathing changed, the steady, rhythmic draw and release becoming the long inhalation that signaled a gradual return to awareness. The arm around my waist pulled me closer, though I couldn't be sure if it was deliberate or unconscious. There was no question, though, that the gentle press of his lips to the back of my shoulder was—unlike the goose bumps it raised—voluntary.

He nuzzled my neck, the coarseness of his stubbled jaw sending a shiver down my spine and rousing me to full consciousness. The tip of his thumb circled my nipple, and my breath caught when his lips pressed against the back of my shoulder once more.

I caressed the back of his hand and fidgeted again, this time to get closer to his body.

"Mmm, didn't get enough last night?" he murmured against my skin.

"Of course I did," I said. "But now it's morning. Sort of."

He laughed. "So the counter starts over when the sun comes up?"

"Yes, it does." *And how long has it been since I've been with a man worth waking up in the middle of the night to fuck? God, yes, I'm in heaven.*

"But the sun hasn't come up yet."

"So do you want to wait until it does?"

"No. Just saying." He kissed the side of my neck. "Tell me what you want."

"I want…" I shivered as his soft goatee and coarse stubble brushed my skin. "I want you to put a condom on."

"Right now?" he murmured. He trailed light fingertips down my side. "What if I want to tease you first?"

"Then that'll be that much longer before you get to fuck me, won't it?"

His hand stopped. "Hmm. Good point. Don't move." He rolled away, and I laughed.

I sat up beside him. "Hey, aren't you supposed to say it's worth the wait, or you want to turn me on first, or some gentlemanly thing like that?"

"Probably." The nightstand drawer opened. Closed. "But it's way too early in the morning, and I'm way too horny to be a gentleman." Foil ripped.

"Hmm, so you turn into a caveman after midnight?"

"That depends." He grabbed my hair and pulled it back hard enough to make me gasp. My nipples tingled, and I bit my lip to suppress a whimper. Growling in my ear, he said, "Do you want the gentleman or the caveman right now?"

"That depends," I said, struggling to find my breath. "Which one will get his cock into me faster?"

"I like the way you think. Now get on your hands and knees." Not that I had much of a choice; he tightened his fist in my hair and twisted it, guiding me into the position he wanted. He forced me onto my forearms. My hard nipples brushed the sheet, and I bit my lip, holding my breath and struggling not to cry out from the sheer anticipation.

He didn't keep me waiting long. He released my hair, grabbed my hips, and in a heartbeat was all the way inside me. That first thrust was always breathtaking, and this time was no exception, but he didn't give me a chance to get used to him before he went straight to hard, violent fucking. From half-asleep and exhausted to...*this*.

"Oh, God, that's amazing," I moaned.

"You're telling me." His thrusts and sharp breaths punctuated his words. Then, completely out of the blue, he slapped my ass hard enough to make my skin and eyes sting, and the pillow bunched in my clawing hands. There was no way in hell his neighbors slept through *that* cry.

"Like that?" he asked.

"Yes," I whimpered, almost sobbing. He did it again. And again. Every time he did it, he sent me higher, the mix of pain and pleasure driving me out of my mind. I wanted to tell him to fuck me harder, to beg him to hold on to my hips and give me everything he had, but the words wouldn't come.

I braced myself against the headboard and slammed back against him. It only took two thrusts like that before Austin took over, fucking me so hard it hurt. I screwed my eyes shut, hot tears sliding down my face, and surrendered. It was usually impossible for me to come from this alone, but that orgasm wasn't stopping for anyone or anything.

I released a breathless cry. "My hair... Austin, my..."

He seized my hair and jerked it back, and in seconds, my entire body shuddered with the force of my release. Austin didn't slow down, didn't let go of my hair, didn't let up in the slightest, just kept right on fucking me as hard and fast as he could while I let go.

"That's it, baby," he said, panting. "Come for me. Let me...let me feel you... Oh, fuck, that's..." He took one last thrust and moaned. Shuddered. Collapsed over me.

Together, we sank all the way down to the bed. Austin pulled out but otherwise didn't move. He held himself up on shaking arms to keep from putting his full weight on me, but his warm skin was still against mine. He touched his forehead to the back of my neck, his sharp huffs of breath cooling the sweat between my shoulder blades.

"I thought you were tired," I slurred.

"I was." He kissed the base of my neck. "Kind of hard not to get turned on with a sexy, naked woman in my bed, though."

"Well, any time you feel the need to wake up and throw me around like that, do feel free."

He laughed and dropped another kiss on my skin. "I'll keep that in mind." With a quiet groan, he pushed himself up off me and got out of bed to get rid of the condom. Moments later, he returned, and we settled in to go back to sleep.

Lying beside me now, he was gentle as could be. His fingers laced between mine against my chest, and his body molded against my own. Warm and satisfied beside him, I didn't even try to keep fatigue from taking over.

It was closing in on him too.

"I just can't get enough of you," he slurred. "I have to warn you. In a few hours, I'll probably want to fuck you all over again."

"Mmm, promise?"

He kissed the back of my shoulder. "Will you hold me to it if I do?"

"Mm-hmm."

"Then get some sleep," he whispered. "You've got a busy morning ahead of you."

I managed a sleepy laugh. Then, wrapped in his arms, I drifted back to sleep.

At some point, the sun came up, and eventually, we joined it, dragging our aching selves out of bed.

After we'd shared a long, three-orgasm shower, Austin let me borrow one of his T-shirts. He put on a pair of jeans, and we went out to the kitchen. I supposed there was no sense getting completely dressed. I had a funny feeling we'd just end up taking our clothes off again before long anyway.

It was rapidly becoming clear there was no bad look for Austin. He looked great when he was suave and sexy in a suit, casual and laid back in jeans, and now, disheveled and sleepy-eyed with a shadow of stubble along his sharply angled jaw. He was probably one of those guys who could dig up an old prom or yearbook picture a decade later and not be embarrassed by it. Bastard.

He made some coffee, and after it was poured, we both leaned against the counter and sipped it in silence. It didn't take a brain surgeon to figure out the question hanging in the air between us: where the hell did we go from here?

Austin set his coffee cup on the counter with a dull tap. "I'm sure I don't have to tell you that this could get a bit complicated."

I laughed. "Oh, no, you don't have to tell me."

"So." He swallowed hard. "What do we do?"

"Run off to Vegas, elope, and let the fallout land where it will?"

He chuckled. "Oh, yeah, that sounds like a *great* idea."

"It was a thought," I said. "Anyway, I'm honestly not sure."

"Whatever we decide to do," he said, both his tone and expression turning serious, "I have to make it clear up front—I can't quit my job."

I nodded. "I know. I understand."

"But, are you okay with seeing someone in my line of work, knowing what I'm doing?"

I said nothing for a moment. Then, "Would you be offended if I said it might take some getting used to?"

"Not at all." He ran his fingers through my hair. "In fact, I'd be a little concerned if it didn't."

"I think I can handle it, though," I said. "Seems like it's part and parcel to dating you. So it's worth a try."

Austin laughed halfheartedly and looked into his coffee cup. "That's easy to say now. When it's been a few months of having my work cell phone ring at weird times, or you being at home while I'm working..." He shrugged, and his cheeks colored. "You might not be so enthusiastic about it."

"The same could be said for when the novelty wears of having my kids call while we're out, having to schedule and reschedule when one of them gets sick, that kind of thing."

"So we work around it. Do the best we can." He put his hands on my hips. "I have no idea if we can make this work. But maybe if we're both patient with each other's circumstances, we can at least have some fun with it for a while."

Resting my forearms on his shoulders and lacing my fingers together behind his neck, I said, "I think it's worth a try."

"One thing to consider, though," he said, "is that if it lasts, that's when things could get really complicated. I mean, what if your ex-husband finds out about me? I don't want this causing problems with him or you taking a chance on losing your kids."

I chewed my lip. "I never introduce someone to my kids until we've been dating for a while, so it's not like he'll be able to get on my case about that. So let's just see where things go, and we'll play it by ear."

"But even if I don't meet the kids." He scowled. "People have some weird preconceived notions about people like me. I'd be scared to death of him finding out you were dating me and flipping out."

"Don't worry about him. He'll—"

"I am worried about him, though." He pursed his lips. "I've seen what this kind of thing can do to people's lives if it gets out. For whatever reason, society still thinks all things sexual are evil, and those of us who make money off it?" He grimaced and shook his head.

"I know," I said. "But we'll be fine, at least for now. It'll probably just mean we don't see much of each other during the weeks when I have the kids. I mean, if you're okay with that."

"Oh, yeah, of course," he said. "That's no problem at all. You're not going to offend me by calling the shots with your kids, Jocelyn."

"I just don't want you to think I'm putting you last."

"You're not," he said. "You're putting me second to your kids, as well you should. Especially when you only get them every other week, I'm not going to take that time away from you."

"Thank you," I whispered.

"So I guess we take things a day at a time," he said, tucking a loose strand of hair behind my ear, "and we'll see where things go. I can't promise it'll be easy dating someone in my line of work, though. Not even close."

"I'm willing to give it a try and see what happens."

He smiled. "You're a very, very rare breed of woman, believe me."

"I don't know if I'd go that far."

"Trust me." He cupped my jaw in one hand and wrapped the other arm around my waist. "You are. You're one of the few who'll actually take the time to see me as something other than a whore."

I rested my hands on his shoulders. "And you're one of the few who doesn't keep me at arm's length because I'm a single mom."

He held me closer to him. "At arm's length is the last place I'd keep you, babe." He kissed me lightly, then dipped his head to kiss my neck. "In fact, you know what I really want to do right now?"

Pressing my hips against his, I said, "I think I can guess."

A breath of laughter warmed my skin. "I'm that easy to read, am I?"

"Yes, you are."

His lips traveled, kiss by soft kiss, up the side of my neck. "So do you have plans for the rest of the day?"

Tilting my head to the side, I bit my lip as his stubble brushed my skin. "Not until I pick up the kids tonight."

"Got time to go back in the bedroom for a while?"

"I have plenty of time for that."

Chapter Twelve

Neither of us expected this relationship to be simple, and it wasn't.

We did the best we could, though. We took lunch together whenever our schedules allowed, especially during the weeks when the kids stayed with me. On those nights, if Austin didn't have to work, we always sent a text or called just to say good night. If his job kept us apart on a given evening, and it often did, he'd send a good-night text when he got home, but it was usually quite late, so he didn't call.

It became a running joke to see whose cell phone would be the next to interrupt our time together. If it was mine, at least I could usually deal with whatever my kids needed without having to cut the evening short to attend to them. If it was Austin's, it depended on which phone. His personal phone could usually be ignored. A call on the other cell was almost inevitably followed by an apologetic look, a kiss good night, and a promise to make it up to me the next night. A promise he always fulfilled and then some.

The first few times he had to leave for an impromptu call from a client, it was too weird for words. I spent the rest of the evening imagining what he was doing and with whom, and I questioned, more than once, if I could really do this. It was his job, though. Nothing more. I quickly learned to just not think about it when he was working. He didn't tell me the things that went on. I didn't ask, and I did the best I could to keep my imagination from running away with me.

Austin wasn't defined by his line of work, though, and neither was our relationship. In between all those odd moments that were unique to a situation like ours were plenty of the normal things. Rented movies flickering unwatched on the television screen while we paid more attention to each other on the sofa. Playing and flirting in the kitchen when we were *supposed* to be cooking together. Clinging to my coffee cup at work because we'd been up until three in the morning just talking in bed.

It was a normal, everyday relationship with normal, everyday things. Like, say, the inevitable meeting of the parents.

My folks lived several states away, but his were local. When his elder sister was in town after Austin and I had been dating for a while, he invited me along to dinner at their parents' house.

"I'm assuming they don't know what you do for a living?" I asked on the way over.

He laughed. "My mother would be facedown in her soup and stone dead before I could finish saying 'I'm a whore.'"

"Yeah, I suppose that would be an awkward conversation."

"You could say that." He sighed and shook his head as he turned off the main road into a quaint little development. "My parents are way too conservative for that. Honestly, my mom probably doesn't even know what an escort is, and they'd both have heart failure if they knew what I do."

"So what do you tell them, then?"

"I keep it simple, keep it vague, and change the subject as often as possible."

"Oh, come on, really?"

He laughed. "Okay, not quite." He turned down another road, this time leading us into a small cul de sac. "They just think my design work gets me by. At least then I don't feel like I'm completely lying to them. Just stretching the truth a bit."

"Under the circumstances, I think you can be forgiven."

He shot me a sidelong glance. "Oh, can I?"

"Yes." I eyed him. "But just this once."

"You're *so* kind."

He parked in front of an immaculately well-maintained colonial-style house. Manicured lawn, beds full of colorful flowers, and trimmed rosebushes.

On the way up the brick walkway, Austin rested a gentle hand on the small of my back. "Sure you're ready for this?"

Walking up the porch steps and past the fluttering American flag, I nodded. "Question is, are you?"

"Of course I am." He kissed my cheek. "I know these people. You don't know what you're getting yourself into."

"I know you," I said. "I think I'll be fine."

He laughed and opened the front door. "Mom? Dad?" he called down the hall.

"In here." A woman's voice came from elsewhere. While Austin and I took off our shoes and coats, the source of the voice stepped around a corner.

"Hey, Mom," Austin said.

"Come here, baby." She put her arms out. "Give your mama a hug."

He groaned like a petulant kid. "Do I have to?"

"Don't make me get the frying pan."

"Okay, okay." He hugged his mother, then gestured at me. "Mom, this is Jocelyn, my girlfriend."

"Very nice to meet you," she said. "You can call me Sharon."

"Nice to meet you too," I said.

"It's been far too long since this one's brought a girl home." She shot her son a disapproving look.

"Yeah, yeah, yeah." He rolled his eyes, and she smacked his arm.

To me, she said, "Why don't we go in the living room and have a seat?" She gestured for us to follow her. Over her shoulder, she said, "Dad's just made a run to the store, and Shelby isn't here just yet, but they should both be along shortly."

In the living room, we sat on the couch, and Austin draped his arm around my shoulders.

"So where did the two of you meet?" his mother asked, easing herself into one of two overstuffed recliners.

"Through a friend," Austin said without a hint of irony. "She thought we'd have a thing or two in common, so she hooked us up."

I smothered a laugh. "Perceptive."

"Well, it's about time, I say," Sharon said. "Has he told you how long it's been since he's brought a woman home to meet us?" She clicked her tongue. "Years, honey. I was starting to wonder if he just had a boyfriend he was too embarrassed to bring home."

"*Mother*."

"Oh, honestly." She made a dismissive gesture. "Dad and I wouldn't have cared if you had. We just wondered why you were hiding him."

"Besides the fact that there wasn't a 'him' to hide?" Austin rolled his eyes.

"Well, I know that *now*, but I've been wondering." To me she said, "This one was quite the ladies' man in high school. Has he told you about that?"

Austin grimaced, his cheeks glowing bright red. I patted his thigh and laughed.

"No, I can't say he has," I said.

"Oh, my goodness." Sharon clicked her tongue. "The girls stood in line to go to prom with him."

"*Did* they, now?" I looked at him, inclining my head. "You mean to tell me you had girls lined up around the block?"

Austin gestured dismissively. "It wasn't quite like that."

"It was so," his mother said. "Why else would you have to ask 'which one?' whenever we told you a girl had called?"

"Yeah, Austin." I struggled to contain my laughter. "Why *would* you have to ask that?"

He let out a huff of breath. "It *wasn't* like that."

Sharon started to speak, but a car outside turned all of our heads.

"That would be your sister." Sharon got up. "You two sit tight. I'll go let her in."

After she'd left the room, I looked at him. "So were you really—"

"No, I wasn't." Our eyes met. His cheeks darkened. "Okay, maybe a little."

"Manwhore."

He snorted, and though we both tried to keep our composure, we couldn't help laughing.

"Okay, okay, what's so funny?" said a woman who I assumed to be Austin's sister.

"We were just laughing at that piece of shit you call a car," Austin said, nodding toward the driveway.

"What?" She smirked. "This from the boy who's still driving a car from the twentieth century?"

"Whatever." Austin got up and stepped around the coffee table to embrace his sister.

"God, I've missed you," she said. "It's good to see you."

"You too." He released her and nodded toward me. "This is Jocelyn, my girlfriend. Jocelyn, this is my sister, Shelby."

"Nice to meet you." I stood to shake her hand over the coffee table.

"Likewise," Shelby said. We all took our seats, Shelby occupying the other recliner.

"You didn't bring the kids this time?" Austin said.

She shook her head. "Just here on business, and I didn't want to take them out of school for a week."

"Aw, come on," he said. "You didn't bring them the last three times either."

"Please, Mom's already given me hell for not bringing them." Shelby eyed her mother.

Sharon shrugged. "Well, you're the one who didn't bring my grandchildren with you again, so you know you're going to hear about it."

"Fine, next time I come out, I'll bring them with me." Shelby looked at Austin. "And you and Mom can sort out who's babysitting while I'm doing work-related crap, even if *you* never actually end up babysitting them."

"Austin can come see them all he wants," Sharon said. "But they're staying with me. Grandmother's privilege."

"Yeah, you *would* hog them," Austin muttered. We exchanged glances. It struck me as sad that even though his mother and sister knew he adored those kids, the reason he'd never actually babysit them was because that would mean being alone with them.

"So, Jocelyn," Shelby said. "What do you do?"

"I work in advertising," I said. "Nothing all that exciting. Client account management, that kind of thing."

"Hey, it pays the bills, right?" Shelby smiled.

"That's the important part," I said. "And it's really not a bad job. I like what I do. It's just not terribly interesting to anyone outside of advertising."

"I can relate to that," Shelby said. "I could probably bore you into a coma with some of the things I deal with on a daily basis. And speaking of boring as hell, what are you doing for work these days, Austin?"

Without missing a beat, he said, "Selling my body to desperate women."

"Wow," Shelby deadpanned. "If they're buying, they *must* be desperate." She looked at me. "No offense."

I snorted with laughter. Austin and I exchanged knowing looks. If she only knew.

"You two," their mother said, rolling her eyes. She pushed herself out of her recliner. "I'm going to go check on dinner. Can I trust you all to stay out of trouble?"

"Yes, Mom," both siblings said.

"So, where's Zach tonight?" Shelby asked after Sharon had gone.

"Zach's our younger brother," Austin said to me. To his sister, he said, "When I talked to him earlier in the week, he said he had plans with Hannah all weekend."

"Oh, *there's* a shock," Shelby said with enough venom to announce she wasn't fond of the woman in question.

Austin stiffened. "Uh, they are dating, you know. That sometimes entails spending time together, even when one's sister does come to town on a moment's notice."

"Yeah, but that woman's just using him." Shelby's lips contorted with disgust. "Drives me crazy."

"Hannah?" Austin cocked his head. "She seems like a nice girl to me."

"Yeah, we'll see how long that lasts once she gets what she wants from him," Shelby said.

Austin raised an eyebrow. "And that is?"

Shelby sneered. "A ring and someone to provide for her kids."

"What?" Austin snorted. "Come on, she's not like that."

"Austin, Zach is loaded," Shelby said. "He's got a good job in a rock-solid industry, and she's waiting tables. Don't tell me she's looking at him with anything other than diamonds and dollar signs in her eyes."

I gritted my teeth.

"So, what? Since she's a single mother, she's a damned gold digger?" Austin said.

Shelby shrugged. "Look, pardon me if I question her motives. She needs a dad for her kids, so—"

"Is their father out of the picture?" I asked.

Shelby furrowed her brow, then shrugged again. "I don't know if he is or not, but—"

"Well, if he's still in the picture, is she really looking to replace him?" I said.

Austin put his hand on my knee. It wasn't a warning squeeze to tell me to back off, just a gentle touch.

"Why else would she be looking for a husband?" Shelby said.

I forced back the anger that rose in my throat. "There are other reasons for a single mother to date and remarry, you know. Like the same reasons *other* single women date and marry."

Shelby's eyebrows jumped. "Okay, I suppose there's that. But any man she marries is going to be an instant dad, and I don't like seeing my brother being sweet-talked into—"

"He's a grown adult, Shel," Austin said. "I'm sure he can see what he's getting into. If he's comfortable being their stepdad and happy with the idea of being her husband, then..." He trailed off and shrugged. "More power to him, I say."

"I still think he's going to get screwed," she said. "Maybe I'm just jaded from experience, but most of the single moms my male friends have hooked up with have been gold-digging whores who just want someone to replace their kids' deadbeat dads. I have yet to meet one who *isn't*."

Austin squeezed my leg, and I wasn't sure if it was to restrain me or himself.

"Well, in that case." I rose. Austin looked at me, eyes wide with alarm, when I extended my hand across the coffee table to his sister. "Evidently we haven't been properly introduced. I'm Jocelyn, and I'm a single mom of two who makes her own money, has her own house, and has no desire to replace their father. I also have the audacity to go out on dates once in a while because I might be tired of being alone after seven years."

Jaw slack, she stared wide-eyed at me and shook my hand. I took my seat again. Awkward silence hung between the three of us for a long moment before Sharon called from the other room.

"Austin, Shelby, would you two mind helping your father bring the groceries in?"

They both jumped to their feet, probably as eager as I was to be anywhere but here, and I followed, if only to see if Sharon needed help in the kitchen. On the way out of the room, though, Shelby stopped me.

"Listen," she said. "I think we got off on the wrong foot. I had no idea you were a single mom."

"Sounds like you aren't too thrilled with women like me," I said, almost snarling.

She looked at the floor between us. "I know, and I apologize. The thing is, I've known a few guys who've gotten screwed, and I..." She shook her head. "Really, I apologize. I was out of line. Could we start over?"

I wasn't quick to forgive those who judged me for being a single parent, but I figured I could give her another chance, if only for the sake of keeping the peace while Austin and I were here.

"Yeah, okay." I shifted my weight. "We can start over."

She exhaled. "Thank you. I'm really sorry. I don't think I've had my foot quite that far down my own throat in a long time."

I laughed. "It happens to the best of us."

"I suppose it does." She smiled. "Okay, so, since my brother never brings women around this house, I have to know." She lowered her voice. "Just how serious are things with him?"

Shrugging, I tucked a strand of hair behind my ear. "Oh, we're taking things slow. He hasn't even met my kids yet."

"They'll love him." She beamed. "I didn't bring mine with me on this trip, but he is so, *so* good with them."

"I'm hoping to introduce them eventually," I said. "Just seeing where things go for now. Don't want to get their hopes up or anything." *And there's the small matter of what your brother really does for a living, and how my ex-husband might be less than thrilled...*

Dropping her voice to a conspiratorial whisper, she said, "You must have made an impression, though. I mean, he has to know that now that you've shown your face to Mom, he isn't going to hear the end of it until he puts a ring on your finger."

My cheeks burned. "I don't know if we're going down *that* road any time soon." *Is it wrong of me to wish we could?* I banished that thought as quickly as it had come.

"Well, keep an eye on Mom, then," she said. "She'll probably be naming your kids before dinner's over." Her teeth snapped shut, and her cheeks darkened. "I mean, I'm not trying to imply... It—" She closed her eyes and let out a breath. "I'm really on a roll today, aren't I?"

I laughed. "It's okay, I know what you meant."

Austin appeared in the doorway. "You two aren't talking about me, are you?"

"Of course we are," Shelby said. "Someone has to warn her about you." She looked at me and deadpanned, "You know he used to be a stripper, right?"

"What?" I glared at Austin. "You told me you only danced like that for me."

"Oh, Jesus." Shelby rolled her eyes and exhaled sharply. "You two were *made* for each other." She patted my arm. "Consider yourself warned." She brushed past him, both siblings elbowing each other before she disappeared into the kitchen.

Austin looked at me. "Is it safe to assume you two aren't going to claw each other's faces off?"

"Yeah, we're good." I eyed him. "Even if you did abandon me with her."

He put his hands up. "Hey, I thought you were right behind me. I didn't realize you two were in here."

"Uh-huh."

"Oh, come on," he said. "Like I'd leave you with a member of my own gene pool. Worst-case scenario, assuming you two didn't have a catfight, was her telling you all the things I don't want you knowing about me."

I snorted. "Like what? Your job?"

"*Jocelyn.*" He shot me a playful glare.

"Kidding, kidding."

"You'd better be."

"Or what?"

He snaked an arm around my waist and pulled me to him. "Or I might have to put you over my knee and leave a handprint or two on your ass tonight."

"Ooh, well if you're going to put it like *that*..."

"Brat." He kissed me lightly.

"So were you really a stripper?"

"Please. I may be a shameless whore, but I do have some standards."

"And those standards preclude dressing as a cop and shaking your booty with twenty dollar bills sticking out of your drawers?"

"Yes. Yes, they do."

"Now, now, Austin." I inclined my head and raised my eyebrows but kept my voice quiet. "You're not discriminating against other kinds of sex work, are you?"

He grinned. "No, just saying I wouldn't be caught dead doing that particular variety."

"You sure?" I gestured toward the front door. "I have a couple of twenties in my purse."

"Uh-huh." He kissed me lightly, then turned me around and nudged me toward the kitchen, following it up with a gentle swat on the rear.

I looked over my shoulder and winked at him.

Austin just laughed.

Chapter Thirteen

When my cell went off around eleven thirty one Friday night, a jolt of panic surged through me. I lunged for the coffee table to get my phone, certain it was Michael calling to tell me disaster had struck our kids somehow.

The LCD screen offered both relief and confusion when a single word appeared:

Austin.

That was strange. He had a client tonight. He never called on those nights, just texted to say good night. What on earth was he doing calling me? *Oh, please tell me he didn't accidentally dial my number at an inopportune moment.* I shuddered. There were things about this arrangement that I could deal with. The thought of actually hearing him with a client? Not so much.

Hoping to God that wasn't the case, I flipped open my phone. No barely muffled moans or squeaking furniture. That was promising.

"Hello?"

"Hey," he said.

"What's up?" I glanced at the clock. "I thought you were booked tonight."

"I was. Just left her pl—" He paused, clearing his throat. "I'm on my way home."

"Getting ready to call it a night, then?"

"Well, sort of." He took a breath. "I, um, I wondered if you wanted some company tonight."

That caught me off guard.

"Uh, I, sure," I said. "I figured you'd be tired, though."

"I'm exhausted. And I can't promise more than just some conversation." He paused again, and when he spoke this time, his voice was softer. "I just really want to see you tonight."

"I'll be up for a while," I said. "Come on over."

"Let me swing by my place and grab a shower," he said. "You sure you don't mind me coming over this late?"

"Not at all."

"See you in a while."

After we'd hung up, I stared at my dormant phone. Of course I didn't mind him coming over. I never did. Still, I was more than a little surprised. He had few complaints about his job, but there were only two things that ever crossed his mind after a session with a client: a shower and sleep.

I tried not to think too much of it. So it wasn't his usual routine? So he wanted to see me in the middle of the night, even if he had neither the desire nor energy for sex? That didn't necessarily mean bad news. I tried to ignore the fact that more than a few "I really want to see you, and it can't wait" evenings in my past had ended with tears and breakups.

It was almost one when the soft hum of an engine crept into the stillness of my street. Headlights came through my front window and arced across the wall, the familiar trajectory signaling that the car in question had pulled into my driveway. The lights dimmed, and the engine quieted, returning the neighborhood to its silent, sleepy darkness.

The car door opened. Closed. Muffled footsteps came up the walk, so I stood and started for the door, pretending not to hear the way my heart pounded in time with his approaching steps.

I opened the front door in the same instant he stepped onto the front porch. I didn't have time for a hello, a thought, or even a breath before he cupped my face in both hands and kissed me. His lips were gentle against mine, but his fingers trembled just enough to betray some undefined desperation, some need I couldn't quite identify. It wasn't the kind of hunger that would have us tearing clothes off and trying to get to the bedroom before desire got the best of us. If anything, the way he kissed me now said *this* was what he wanted. This and nothing more.

I wrapped my arms around him and held on, willing my knees not to buckle. It wouldn't matter if they did, though. He'd have kept me upright just like he kept me breathing right then.

His lips left mine. Opening my eyes, I wondered how long we'd been standing here. I looked up at him in the low light from the single overhead bulb and what little spilled out from the lamp I'd left on in the living room. His hair was damp, and his heavy-lidded eyes looked even more exhausted than he'd sounded on the phone.

"Hey you," I said when my mouth could form words again.

"Hey." He caressed my face. "You don't mind me showing up this late, do you?"

"No, of course not." I ran my fingers through his hair. "But you didn't have to come over tonight if you're this tired."

He smiled. "I didn't have to; I wanted to." He kissed my forehead. "I wanted to see you, and I didn't want to wait until tomorrow."

I gulped. In spite of his kiss and the way he held me out here beneath my porch light, something about this unsettled me. Old habit, I supposed, but if he wasn't here for sex or to end it, then what?

Only one way to find out, though. I gestured into the house, and we separated enough to cross the threshold and close the front door. I leaned against it. Austin looked at me, and there it was again, this time in his eyes, that undefined hunger for...something.

Then it was in his kiss again. Up against the door, one hand caressing my face while the other arm held me close to him, he kissed me like...like...

Fuck, I couldn't put my finger on it. Everything about this was sexual, but not. Quietly passionate, desperately gentle. Every breath was made of desire and...was it?

Relief?

Austin, what's on your mind?

Our lips separated, and our foreheads touched.

"I thought you weren't in the mood for anything," I whispered.

"I'm always in the mood when I'm around you," he said. "And if I wasn't so tired, I would. Believe me, I would."

"But you're..." I paused. With a playful and slightly cautious grin, I said, "So you're just teasing me, then?"

Austin dropped his gaze and swallowed hard. He loosened his embrace. "No, I'm not trying to tease you. I'm sorry, baby. I'm—"

"Don't apologize." I ran my thumb back and forth along his jaw. "Just tell me what you *do* want."

"This." He cupped my face in his hands again. Leaning in, he tilted his head slightly and whispered, "This is exactly what I came for."

He wasn't here to call this off. Of that much, I was certain.

But he held me like a man starved of physical contact. No need to arouse, no need to get hands on bare flesh and seek release. His touch was gentle, his kiss light, and though he didn't make any effort to get past my clothes or find those erogenous zones he'd long ago memorized, he didn't let go either.

Like a man who not only needed to hold, but to be held.

I broke the kiss this time and looked up at him. I reached up to touch his face again, and he closed his eyes, drawing in a long breath as I ran my fingertips over his slightly stubbled jaw.

"You okay tonight?" I asked.

Opening his eyes, he nodded, and the smile that spread across his lips made my knees weak.

"I'm fine." He laughed, his cheeks coloring as he shifted his gaze away. "Probably sounds ridiculous, needing to come over in the middle of the night just—"

"No, not at all. You just seem…" I searched for the words, but when they didn't come, I shook my head. "I don't know. I was just worried something was wrong."

"No, nothing's wrong." He stroked my hair and kissed my forehead. "Nothing at all." He rolled his shoulders and tilted his head back, closing his eyes as he popped a crick out of his neck.

"You sure you're okay?"

He nodded, then laughed shyly. "It's a…you know…physical job."

"I guess it is." I put my arms around him. "I could give you a massage if you think that would help."

"I think it just might." He kissed me. "And even if it doesn't, I'll have your hands on me, so I win either way, right?"

I laughed. "Come on. Let's go upstairs."

Austin smiled. "You're a saint. You know that?"

"We'll see about that." I slipped my hand into his, and we started up the stairs.

"Fair warning," he said. "If I fall asleep, it's not because you're boring me."

"Well, if you do," I said, glancing back at him, "I'll just go to sleep next to you, and we can finish whatever conversation we're having in the morning."

At the top of the stairs, he stopped me, putting his arms around me from behind. Nuzzling my neck, he whispered, "You're sure you don't mind?"

"Have I ever objected to having you in my bed?"

His quiet laugh warmed my skin. "That's true; you haven't. But usually I'm putting out."

I turned around in his arms and grinned. "I think I'll survive if you don't." Trying to look stern, I added, "But just this once."

He chuckled. Then he kissed me lightly, and we continued down the hall to my bedroom. Austin sat on the edge of the bed while I turned away to look through a dresser drawer.

"I'm pretty sure I've got some massage oil around here somewhere," I said. "Give me a minute, and I'll see if I can find it."

"I'm in no hurry. And hell, hand lotion works too."

"Hand lotion works, yes." *Where the hell did I put that stuff? I know I have some. Don't I?* "But if I'm going to do this, I want to do it right."

"Oh, I doubt that'll be a problem." He laughed quietly. "So how do you want me?"

"Naked and covered in chocolate sauce would be fine," I said over my shoulder.

"That could be arranged."

"But not tonight, right?"

"Rain check?"

"Deal. For now, take your shirt off and lay on your stomach." *Damn it, I know I have some oil.* "Assuming that's comfortable?"

"We'll find out, won't we?" Fabric whispered over skin. The hairs stood up on the back of my neck, goose bumps prickling all the way down my spine at the mere knowledge he was now shirtless. Then my mattress creaked just enough to hint at accommodating weight, and I shivered.

I finally found the bottle of massage oil tucked in the back of my lingerie drawer. I pulled it out and turned around.

And stopped. Just for a minute. Just to look.

Because, sweet Jesus, I never tired of the sight of that man, particularly when he was in my bed. Lying like that, on his stomach with his arms folded beneath his head, he *radiated* sex. He still wore his low-slung jeans, and they emphasized his narrow waist while the way he'd folded his arms made his shoulders look even broader. I could have spent half the night tracing his tattoos with my fingertips or even just running my fingers along the grooves between his muscles.

Or, say, giving him a massage.

I knelt beside him on the bed and opened the bottle. "I haven't done this in a while. I might be a bit rusty."

"You're more than welcome to practice all you want on me."

I warmed some of the oil between my hands. "Just figured I should warn you. I'm no expert here." I put my hands on his shoulders.

"Well, now's as good a time as any to—*oh*, wow..." His voice trailed off into a groan when I pressed in the heels of my hands and ran them up either side of his spine.

"Tell me if anything I do hurts," I said.

"Trust me, you're good," he murmured.

For a few minutes, I just let my hands memorize his shape, tracing the contours of his broad shoulders and the sculpted muscles of his back, trailing over his tattoos. I had to resist the urge to let my fingers wander all over the intricate inked lines. There would be time for that later.

As many times as I had been in bed with him, I found myself exploring him as if I'd never touched him before. Just the sight of my own fingertips on his skin mesmerized me, and the warmth of his body in my hands sent shivers through my body. I was glad he faced away from me then so he didn't notice that my nipples had hardened beneath my T-shirt.

Slowly, I pressed harder into his flesh, kneading gently until I found a few rigid knots in his muscles. He tensed when my knuckles dug into a particularly stubborn one.

"Sorry," I whispered, but kept my knuckle against it, pressing into the center of the knot until it began to release. Gradually, the muscle softened, and Austin exhaled.

"Where did you learn to do that?" he breathed.

"I dated a massage therapist once. A few years ago." I found another knot and started working on it.

He took in a sharp hiss of breath, then relaxed when the second knot released. "He taught you well."

"Well, at least he was good at something."

Austin laughed. "Really? Not so great in the sack?"

"To say the least." I ran my hands up and down his back again, easing the ache out of my own muscles before I worked on another sore spot. His oil-moistened skin was like silk beneath my hands; I could have touched him like that for hours.

Austin breathed out. "Well, whatever he did or didn't do, you're absolutely amazing at this."

"I try," I said. "Put your forehead on your hands, so your neck is straight."

He obeyed, and I slid my hands from his shoulders to his neck, letting my fingers go around to the sides of his neck while my thumbs gently kneaded the taut muscles along his spine.

"Good God, that's awesome," he slurred.

After a while, I brought my fingers together on the back of his neck and moved them into his hair, letting them separate around the sides of his head with gentle but firm pressure on his skin. His still-damp hair was cool between my fingers as I gently massaged his scalp. He groaned, and I watched the tension in his shoulders melt away with each circle of my fingertips in his hair.

Then I brought my hands back to his shoulders and kneaded them, digging my fingers in enough to release the tightness without causing him pain. I listened to his breathing, watching how high and how often his ribs expanded when he breathed, adjusting my touch and my speed in response to his cues.

Austin shifted. I thought he was just getting comfortable, so I lifted my hands off him, but the muscles in his back rippled as he turned over. I moved over him, straddling his hips and leaning down to kiss him. It was a gentle kiss, just his lips against mine, no sound between us but our slow, steady breathing.

When I sat up a little, he looked up at me, running his fingers through my hair. "I have absolutely nothing left tonight," he whispered. "But I really, really want to touch you."

"I'm not going anywhere."

"Just fair warning," he said. "I don't want you to think I'm teasing you or getting you all worked up for nothing."

Leaning down to kiss him again, I said, "Oh, I wouldn't call this *nothing*."

"Neither would I." His hand slid around my neck and into my hair, his other arm wrapping around me. His tongue gently parted my lips. When his fingers found their way under my shirt and pressed against the small of my back, I couldn't help but release a ragged breath. He hadn't set out to turn me on, and I knew this would be as far as we went tonight, but damn if he didn't have that effect whether he tried to or not.

His other hand went to my waist, and he pushed my shirt up, moving slowly, deliberately, like he wanted to memorize every contour of my body. I sat up and pulled my shirt the rest of the way off, tossing it aside. With a quick motion, I unsnapped my bra and got rid of it too. I started to come back down to him, but he stopped me with a gentle hand on my waist.

"No," he breathed. "Just…stay just like that." He watched his own hands sliding up my waist.

"What is it?"

"I just want to look at you." His fingertips grazed my collarbone, then started back down my chest. His breath caught as he cupped my breasts. "My God, baby..." His thumbs circled my nipples, barely touching my skin but sending a shiver through me.

I closed my eyes and sighed. When I opened them, he looked up at me. He exhaled, letting his gaze wander up and down while his hands did the same.

"I don't know if I've ever told you this, but you're beautiful, Jocelyn," he whispered. "Absolutely beautiful." He released a deep breath, as if the sight of his hands on my body hypnotized him. "Everything about you is just..." He trailed off, his lips still parted like he couldn't find the words. When he did, the single word was barely more than a ragged breath: "*Beautiful.*"

I leaned forward and kissed him. He met my lips gently, putting his arms around me again and holding me close.

Then one hand went from my neck to my chest, and I gasped when he cupped my breast.

"Hmm, look what I've gone and done." He teased my hardened nipple with his thumb. "I said I wouldn't, but I think I've turned you on after all."

"This shouldn't be a surprise," I murmured, trying not to whimper when he pinched my nipple between his thumb and forefinger. "You always turn me on."

"Do I?" He grinned. "Well, I can't possibly leave you turned on without doing something about it. You might burn the place down."

"I thought you were too tired."

"I am." He put his arms around me and rolled me onto my back. "You, however, are not."

"But you—"

"Shh." He propped himself up on one elbow and let his other hand drift down my belly. He unbuttoned my jeans and slowly drew the zipper down. "I'm not about to go to sleep while my girlfriend is wound up and frustrated in the same bed."

"You're such a gentleman."

He laughed, then bent to kiss my neck. "I've been accused of being many things, my dear, but a gentleman is not one of them." His hand slid beneath my jeans and panties. "But any man who'd leave you to your own devices when he could so easily lend a hand?" His fingertips made slow, teasing circles around my clit. "Well, he'd be a right bastard, wouldn't he?"

"Hmm, if I agree with that, will you keep doing what you're doing?"

"I will anyway." He kissed my neck again. Like he always did, he turned my body to liquid with a touch. Fingers on my clit, lips on my skin, and if that wasn't enough, he said, "I couldn't wait until tomorrow to see you." His fingers—first one, then a second—slipped easily into my pussy. "Baby, if you only knew what you do to me." His fingertips found my G-spot, and I whimpered as he added, "I just couldn't wait."

I grabbed his shoulder with one hand, the sheets bunching beside me in the other. "Keep..." I gasped, and my spine lifted off the bed. "Keep doing that."

"Just like this? You're already close, aren't you?" His voice dipped to a low growl. "Fuck, I love that, the way your pussy gets tighter when you're right there."

My vision clouded over. Every inch of my skin tingled, my nerve endings crackled, and I was almost there, almost there. Almost. There.

Right when I teetered on that precipice between holding on and letting go, Austin whispered, "If I were inside you right now, I would fucking *lose* it."

And I did lose it. My lips parted for a cry of ecstasy, but my voice and breath were lodged in my throat, and without a word, without a sound, I came, grabbing on to the sheets and Austin while my body trembled against him. His fingers slowed enough to keep it from getting too intense, but nowhere near enough to let my orgasm recede. He kept me going for the longest time, coaxing wave after wave of unbelievable ecstasy from my clit and G-spot until I begged him to stop.

"Oh, my God," I murmured as he withdrew his fingers. "That's amazing."

He grinned and kissed me lightly. "You're not the only one with a little magic in the hands."

We both laughed. After another gentle kiss, we parted long enough to get rid of our clothes. Then we got back into bed and turned on our sides, and Austin pulled the sheet up over us. Facing each other, we didn't speak for a long time. He watched his fingers run through my hair, probably oblivious to the fact that the two creases between his eyebrows may as well have been a neon sign that said I'M THINKING.

"What's on your mind?" I asked.

He shifted and rested his hand on my arm. "Thinking a little. About why I came here tonight."

Something in my stomach flipped. "You wanted a massage?"

He laughed. "Apparently. I just didn't know it at the time."

"So, why *did* you come over tonight?" I grinned. "Not that your company's unwelcome, of course."

Austin smiled. "Because I wanted to see you." He brushed the pad of his thumb across my cheekbone.

"And you didn't want to wait until tomorrow?"

I half-expected him to laugh and make a playful comment, but his expression remained completely serious when he whispered, "I couldn't wait until tomorrow."

I swallowed hard and absently trailed my fingers up and down his forearm. "You...couldn't?"

"No." His eyes lost focus for a moment. "I guess I've just been doing some thinking, and after..." He paused. "After this evening, I needed to be with you."

"Why?" I raised my eyebrows. "Did something happen?"

"No, no, nothing like that. It was just like any session with any client." He ran his fingers through my hair. "That's just it, actually. I do this all the time, but the longer you and I do this..." He pursed his lips and his eyes lost focus. Finally, he took a breath and looked at me again. "You know, there are people who think with what I do, I'm just giving away something that should be kept between two people." He touched my face. "And that couldn't be further from the truth, honestly."

"How so?"

Austin moistened his lips and watched his fingers play with a strand of my hair. "Yeah, I have sex with other women. But there's... It's..." He released a frustrated breath. "It's just not that simple." His brow furrowed. I didn't speak, instead letting him find the words that eluded him.

Finally, he took a deep breath.

"There's sex, and there's...this." He met my eyes. "Just being with someone like this. This isn't something that can be bought or sold, and I couldn't manufacture it for someone no matter how much they tried to pay me for it." He ran the backs of his fingers down my cheek. "That's why I'm here tonight. Because I needed this. And here, with you, is the only place I can get it." He swallowed hard. "Or give it."

My heart pounded. "So, intimacy, then."

"Yes, intimacy. Exactly." He moistened his lips again and held my gaze. "That's something I only have with you." Before I could speak, his hand slid from my face into my hair, and he kissed me.

Austin was the last man in the universe I should have been like this with. No matter how much I could tune out the rest of the world when we were in bed, that world still existed beyond the bedroom walls, and there were people in it who expected him to put out for pay. Those same people would be horrified to know I felt this way about someone—some*thing*—like him. He was Austin, but he was still Sabian.

This intimate tenderness had all the makings of a long-term relationship, but reality held too many cards that simply wouldn't allow it to happen.

Still, whether it should have been or not, there it was again, that same gentle but desperate kiss we'd shared on the porch and up against the door, only now it made sense. Now I understood what he'd been after, and had I been in his shoes, I'd have driven across town in the middle of the night for it too. Not for *me*, per se, but for this deep intimacy that couldn't be bought, sold, forced, or ignored.

And I couldn't ignore it.

Chapter Fourteen

A week or two later, after a day from hell at my own job, it was my turn to preface a visit with "I might not be good company."

Austin wasn't dissuaded, though. "I promise I'll make it worth your while," he'd said over the phone with that grin in his voice. "*And* I'll cook for you." Now, I'd made some stupid decisions in my life, but passing up an evening of Austin's cooking and whatever else would make it worth my while? Not a chance.

So, after a shower, a change of clothes, and a few deep breaths to settle myself enough to keep any lethal levels of road rage at bay, I drove over to his apartment.

When I walked through his front door, I caught a faint but familiar scent. Something hot. Burning.

Candles.

The light was on in the living room, and there were no candles in sight, but I knew that smell. Grinning to myself as I set my purse down, I wondered what he had up his sleeve.

Austin closed the door and came up behind me, hands on my hips and lips on my neck. "Just the usual bullshit at work?"

"Yeah, you could say that."

"I'd rather fix it." His lips curved into a grin against my skin.

"And I'm sure you've thought of just how to do that, haven't you?"

"I have." He pulled my jacket over my shoulders, fingertips trailing down my arms as he pulled it all the way off. He turned away just long enough to hang it up, then put his arms around my waist and kissed beneath my ear. "And I think you'll enjoy it."

"Of that, I have no doubt," I murmured.

"Do you want a drink first or everything else I have planned?"

"Hmm," I said. "Depends on what the drink is and what you have planned."

"Vodka and whatever I can find to mix with it." He kissed the side of my neck. "Or you can take what's behind door number one."

"What's behind door number one?"

The tip of his tongue made a slow circle below my ear. "You have to pick first." His lips and voice brushed my skin. "The drink or the mystery prize?"

I shivered. "How about a rain check on the drink?"

His fingertips slipped under the back of my shirt. "I was hoping you'd say that."

Turning around in his arms, I kissed him. "So what's behind door number one?"

"You'll see." He gently turned me around again and guided me down the hall, flicking the living room light off behind us. The entire apartment was dark now except for a soft amber glow in the bedroom ahead of me. My heart thudded with every step we took. It didn't take a genius to figure out that whatever Austin had in mind, it would—sooner or later—end in sweat and orgasms. That thought alone was enough to raise my body temperature and negate my entire workday. Curiosity about what *else* he had planned made me tremble with excitement.

Every light in the bedroom was off, but a half dozen or so candles flickered on the dresser and nightstand. The comforter and blanket were already pulled back, the pillows piled neatly on one side of the bed. A bottle of what I assumed to be massage oil sat beside the candles.

"I was thinking," he said against the skin beneath my ear as he reached around to unbutton my blouse, "that you could use a massage."

Right then and there, I nearly melted. "You don't mind?"

"Not in the least. Especially not after the one you gave me." He hooked his fingers under either side of my shirt and drew it over my shoulders and down my arms. "I'm guessing you don't either?"

A breathless laugh did little to mask the shiver that ran up my spine as he trailed his fingertips down my back. A playful retort was right on the tip of my tongue but disappeared when my bra loosened and fell down my arms. I held my breath, expecting his hands over my breasts, but he abruptly broke contact altogether. Fabric rustled behind me, and when his arms went around me—hands cupping my breasts as

I'd anticipated—his bare chest was hot against my back.

I covered his hands with my own, closing my eyes and letting my head fall back against his shoulder while he kissed my neck.

"If this is what happens when I have a bad day," I whispered, "I'll take anything my job can dish out."

"We've barely started." He nipped my shoulder before releasing me. "Let's get the rest of these clothes out of the way so I can do what I promised."

After we'd undressed, he handed me one of the pillows off the bed.

"Lie on your stomach with this under your hips."

I took it but stopped to kiss him first. His hard cock pressed against my hip, and I grinned at him. "So is this a massage or foreplay?"

He laughed, drawing his fingertips up my back. "Who says it can't be both?"

I shivered. He kissed me one last time, then nudged me toward the bed. I did as he asked, lying with the pillow under my hips, and he ran a hand from the small of my back to my shoulders.

"I could just look at you like this all night." His hand drifted back and forth across my shoulders. "Just looking at you..." A single fingertip traced a line down the center of my spine "Touching you..." He bent and kissed the back of my neck. "Thinking about all the ways I'm going to make you come before we're done."

All I could do was breathe.

"And I'll get to that," he said, his voice dropping as it always did when he was turned on. "I'll get to that very, very soon. But first…" He sat up and reached for the bottle of massage oil on the nightstand. The bottle clicked, then again, and after he'd set it down, he sat back again, out of my sight, and the hiss of skin brushing skin gave me goose bumps. I pictured him rubbing his hands together to heat the oil. My skin tingled at the very thought of warm, oiled hands sliding over my tense muscles.

The mattress creaked with shifting weight, and I closed my eyes, expecting his hands at any moment, in any place. When? Where?

What I didn't expect was the soft, tender kiss on the small of my back, his lips and breath warm against my skin. I sucked in a breath, exhaling only when he did, breathing in again when his inhalation cooled the air just above my skin. As he kissed his way up my back, I was more aware than ever of the contours of my own spine: the gentle decline from my lower back before it swept up toward my shoulders, then a subtle downward curve before rising once more to the sensitive place just beneath my hairline.

Then, without a word, he changed position, sitting over me with his knees on either side of my hips, and his oiled hands went to work on my muscles.

I barely felt what he did to my back and shoulders. While his hands melted the tension in my muscles, his erection against the back of my thigh created a whole different kind of tension. The more he touched me, the more I wanted him to keep doing it, but the more I ached for his cock.

His hands glided up my back, making slow, firm circles, and every time his body moved, his hips inched closer to mine. Even as his hands again moved down my spine, working their way to the small of my back, his hips didn't retreat at all.

I shivered.

"Cold?" he asked.

"No, far from it." I moistened my dry lips. "I just really, really like what you're doing."

"You mean this?" His hands left my shoulders and found their place on my lower back again. "Or this?" His lips touched between my shoulder blades again, making me close my eyes and whimper softly. I'd never thought of that spot as an erogenous zone. Maybe it hadn't been before this moment.

"Everything you're doing," I whispered. "I love it."

"Good," he breathed against my back before kissing higher, then higher, still higher, each soft, tender kiss eliciting the same shiver as the last. Maybe the erogenous zone wasn't my skin at all, but his lips. A sexual Midas touch.

His hands moved slowly up my back to my shoulders, just as they had a moment ago, and every nerve ending tingled as if it'd been dormant all along until his fingertips brought it to life. When he made a warm, slow circle with the tip of his tongue at the base of my neck, I shivered. It didn't matter where or how he touched me—the response was the same. When Austin touched me, every nerve in my body may as well have been hardwired straight to my G-spot.

When he paused to reach for the massage oil again, he lifted himself off me, and it was all I could do not to scream for him to come back. *No, you're so close; please don't go away.*

But I bit my tongue. He had something in mind. He knew what he was doing. He'd never disappointed me. Teased me to the brink of madness, yes, but never disappointed.

I thought he'd pick up the bottle of massage oil again, but instead, he went for one of several condoms sitting beside it.

He tore the wrapper. "Don't worry, by the way," he said. "That oil is condom-safe."

"I figured it would be," I slurred.

The bottle clicked. Then once more. He set it down and was over me again.

I expected his warm, slick hands on my back, but it was his cock that I felt first, pressing against my pussy but not going any farther. Then, and only then, his hands resumed their gentle motions on my skin. Every muscle in my body relaxed, but every nerve went on high alert, seeking the delicious sensations that were no more than a well-timed thrust away.

The heels of his hands pressed into my shoulders, and his cock pressed just a little harder against my pussy. I exhaled, whimpering softly.

"You like that?" he whispered, a note of amusement mixing with that low growl of arousal. I nodded.

His hands tightened on my shoulders, and his hips moved, pushing just the head of his cock into me, then withdrawing, then doing it again.

"Now you're just teasing," I said.

"I'm not teasing, I promise. I'm just not rushing." And with that, he slowly slid into me, letting me feel every last inch of him. With my legs together, my pussy seemed tighter and his cock seemed thicker, almost painfully so.

Once he was all the way inside me, his hips stopped, but the heels of his hands kept kneading my back, my shoulders, the sides of my neck. Every time his weight shifted, his cock moved almost imperceptibly inside me, nudging my G-spot just enough to make it impossible for me to breathe. Otherwise, though, he was still. He was simply inside me. Simply *there.*

Every place he touched became erogenous, and I dug my elbows into the bed, pressing back against him, needing him deeper.

The pressure from his hands diminished until they barely touched me, sliding lightly over my oiled skin. Starting at my shoulders, he made featherlight circles, each a little lower than the last until they brushed over the tingling base of my spine. Then they slid onto my sides and down to my hips and there, finally there, he held tighter. Grasping me. Steadying me.

When he started to withdraw, I gasped. He'd been still for so long, simply being inside me without moving, my body didn't want to let him go. My pussy tightened around him, but he continued pulling out, pulling almost all the way out. And there was nothing I could do but let him. Surrender to him. I shuddered, moaning softly when the head of his cock slid past my G-spot.

"Oh my God, Austin," I breathed.

"Baby, you feel so good this way." He slid back in just as slowly. "You're so..." A soft moan. "You're so tight." When he was all the way in, he stopped, releasing a ragged breath. "Do you like it this way?"

"Yes," I moaned, drawing my hips forward to keep him moving. I didn't want him to pull out. I wanted him all the way inside my pussy, but I didn't want him to stop *moving*. "I love it. I *love* it."

"Good." He moved a little faster now, and in this position, I was powerless to do anything except lie there and love it.

I reached forward to grab the slats on the headboard. I couldn't hold on to him, but I needed something to keep me here. I'd never felt anything like this. He was inside me, over me, touching me, fucking me. His cock moved as slowly as his hands, overwhelming my senses with...*him*.

He slowed down and shifted his weight, his hands releasing my hips and moving to my back again.

"I wish you could see what I see right now," he said, barely whispering. His hands ran down my sides—just touching now, no longer massaging—and he released a hiss of breath when he pulled out slowly, then pushed back in. "Jesus, baby, your body is fucking beautiful."

Fingertips trailed up the center of my spine, and I arched my back, seeking more.

One hand lifted off me. Skin whispered across sheets. First his hand, then his forearm, came to rest on the bed beside me. The other arm did the same, and his slick fingers hooked over my elbows, and he used my arms as leverage as he moved faster.

His breath warmed the back of my neck, but the touch of his lips to my skin still startled me. His thrusts were deep, urgent, his hands tightening around my arms every time he drove himself into me.

"Oh God, Austin," I moaned. "Oh God, you feel so good…" I probably sounded on the verge of tears, and maybe I was, but all I knew was how close I was to falling completely apart.

He abruptly released my arm and grabbed the same headboard slat I was holding, then did the same with his other hand. A growl emerged from somewhere deep within him, and he fucked me even harder, the bed creaking in time with his rapid, desperate rhythm. His breath came in short, sharp gasps against the back of my neck, and through the tears welling up in my eyes, I could barely see how much his arms tensed with each thrust.

Everything about this was surreal. Overwhelming. Contradictory. Primal and tender. Painful and perfect. Savage and sensual.

Hints of flickering amber candlelight reflected off the sheen of sweat and oil on his skin, and his muscles rippled and quivered. His masculine scent mingling with the sweet smell of massage oil made me tremble, and no sound was ever more erotic than the bed frame groaning in time with the sharp whispers of breath beside my ear.

Every stroke drove me closer yet seemed to keep my climax that much further out of my reach. Closer and further, too much and not enough, *can't wait and can't take it…*

"Austin." I drew in a breath and closed my eyes, gripping the headboard for dear life and using it to push back against him, desperate for more. "Oh God, Austin..." I couldn't continue because I couldn't release my breath.

"Let yourself go, baby," he whispered. "Don't hold back. I want"—his voice faltered—"I want to feel you..."

And I let go.

Of my breath. Of the headboard. Of everything.

With a throaty roar that collapsed into a soft whimper, he shuddered against me.

His chest rested against my back, though he kept most of his weight on his elbows. After a moment, his hands released the headboard slats in the same instant his lips released a long, ragged breath.

"Feel better?" he murmured, kissing the back of my neck.

"God, yes."

His soft laughter simultaneously warmed and cooled my damp skin. "I thought that might help." He pushed himself up and pulled out slowly. While he took care of the condom, I rolled onto my side, brushing a few strands of hair out of my face. Feel better? Oh, he was damn right I felt better.

Austin joined me in bed again, pulling the sheet up over us and draping his arm over my waist. Neither of us spoke. In the soft, flickering candlelight, we just looked at each other.

Maybe it was the different lighting, maybe a few months had dulled my memory, but I couldn't put the face looking back at me now in the doorway of that hotel room the night we met. I'd paid someone for a couple of nights in bed, a clandestine role-playing game in my office, and somehow that man was now *this* man. Sabian the stranger to Austin the lover.

Of course I'd known for some time this was more than just sex for cash, but tonight it felt...different. Those first nights, I'd seen him as someone who would be there and gone. Ships passing in the night. Tonight, here in his bed and his arms, he looked like a more permanent fixture. Someone who'd be around for a while, at least. There was no ticking clock waiting to see him out, no need for me to drink him in and memorize him so I'd someday look back and still remember his face, because he wasn't going anywhere.

Austin touched my face, the vague slickness of his fingertips reminding my nerve endings of his mind-bending massage. I closed my eyes, and a second later, his lips met mine. I wondered if he could fathom the effect his kiss had on me, what these slow, tender movements did to my pulse. No one else's kiss had ever reduced the universe to the space we occupied. Something like this simply couldn't be wrong.

The more I thought about it, the more I realized just how much I wanted Austin in my life. Right or wrong, I wanted this to be more than a fling, and if it had any chance of lasting beyond that, there were things that had to be addressed. Complications that couldn't be ignored.

Austin looked into my eyes and caressed my cheek. "You okay?"

I nodded.

"You're tense again all of a sudden," he said. "Something else on your mind?"

"Yeah." I swallowed hard. "Yeah, there is." I chewed the inside of my cheek. "This is going to sound crazy, but I want to tell my ex-husband about you."

His brow furrowed. "Your ex? Like, tell him that we're dating? Or what I do?"

"Both."

Austin's lips parted. "How do you think he'll take it?"

"I don't know." I sighed. "To be honest, I have no idea. But I think it would be better for him to know in the beginning, for us to be completely up front about it, rather than have him find out later." I took a breath. "Like, have him find out *after* you've met my kids."

He blinked. "Are you serious?"

"Yes," I whispered. "I want you to meet my kids."

A smile played at his lips, but it didn't last. "I do want to meet them, but are you sure this is the way to go? He might flip out."

"I know. But he'd be even more upset if I told him or he found out later. I'd rather keep everything on the table and out in the open than have to explain it to him after the fact."

"Understandable," he said, "but what if he decides to take you to court or something? I don't want you losing your kids because of me, babe."

"He won't take them," I said. "He's more reasonable than that."

"Yeah, but are you sure this is a risk you want to take? I don't want to lose you, but if you stand to lose *them*..."

The truth was I knew it was a risk. A small one, but a risk nonetheless. The prospect scared the hell out of me, but what could I do?

"Jocelyn," he whispered, touching my face, "I don't want you risking custody of your kids for me."

I put my hand over his. "Then what do you suggest? If we're going to continue seeing each other—and I want to—we'll have to address this sooner or later."

He was quiet for a moment. "It's your call. You know him better than I do. But I know from experience, this kind of thing doesn't usually go over well."

"I don't expect him to be thrilled with it, but he'll deal with it." Squeezing his hand, I said, "I know him. This is the best way to go where he and the kids are concerned."

"So how would we go about this?" he asked. "Would you want to talk to him first, then have him meet me?"

"I was thinking it would be best if I meet him somewhere, talk to him, and have you join us. That way he has time to chew on it but doesn't have time to go sleep on it and let himself get worked up after conjuring up some stereotypical image of you."

Austin laughed. "Yeah, I suppose that would be a bad idea." He raised his head and leaned in to kiss me gently. "Are you sure about this?"

"If we're going to do this, then let's just jump in with both feet and quit pretending we're not doing it." I took a breath. "I'm not giving you an ultimatum or anything, Austin. I just—I don't want to put this off." I ran my fingers through his damp hair. "I'm not ashamed of what you are, and I don't want to hide you."

Austin avoided my eyes for a moment. Then he swallowed hard. "What if he objects to me meeting the kids?"

I exhaled. There were only so many options if that happened. One option in particular would be painful for both of us.

"We'll cross that bridge if and when we get there," I whispered.

Austin nodded slowly. "If that's what you want, then…go ahead and talk to him. You tell me where to be and when, and I will."

"Thank you," I whispered.

He smiled but said nothing. Instead he kissed me again. We drew it out this time, and as I wrapped my arms around him and let him guide me onto my back, the knot in the pit of my stomach loosened a little. Michael had to see there was more to Austin than his job. He had to. It would be a shock, of that I had no doubt, but once he met Austin and talked to him and saw he was a normal human being, he'd be fine.

Right?

Chapter Fifteen

I met Michael at a café downtown on Saturday afternoon. Austin would join us after half an hour. I figured that would be enough time to drop the bomb on Michael, let him chew on it for a little while, but not give him enough time to get himself worked up and freaked out. Both men were chronically on time, so at least that part of my plan was bulletproof.

One o'clock, Michael.

One thirty, Austin.

As was my custom, I got there early, finding a table for three that was visible from the doorway but put some space between us and other patrons. While I waited for my ex-husband, I ordered a soda but barely touched it. My fingers tapped out an uneven tempo on the blue Formica, keeping time with my scattered, racing thoughts.

It wasn't that I doubted what I was doing. If Austin and I were to pursue our relationship any further, then this was a necessary evil. I couldn't risk Michael finding out after the kids had already been around Austin.

But what if he did flip out? What if he threatened to take the kids or refused to agree to Austin meeting them? Of course I could introduce a boyfriend to my kids without my ex's consent, but in *this* situation, Michael held the cards. If he refused to allow Austin near our children, then what?

"Your Honor, I want an injunction to keep my ex-wife's boyfriend from our children."

"And why is that, Mr. Rhodes?"

"Because he's an admitted prostitute."

"Is this true Ms. Rhodes?"

"Uh..."

I shuddered.

Austin would never ask me to choose between the kids and him. There was a possibility Michael *would* ask me to choose between them and Austin, though. My stomach turned at the very thought. Austin would understand if I had to make that choice, but damn it would hurt if things came down that.

The sleigh bells above the door jingled, and I looked up as my ex-husband stepped into the restaurant. He waved, then started across the floor. My heart pounded. How ironic; this was probably the first time in a decade his presence had affected my blood pressure like this. There was a time when he had made my heart flutter with something very, very different. That feeling was reserved for someone else now.

"Hey," he said, leaning down to kiss my cheek as he sometimes did. "You haven't been waiting long, have you?"

"Oh, no, you're right on time." I smiled. "I was here early."

He laughed and took a seat. "You? Early? Oh, there's a shock."

"I know—stop the presses."

We exchanged smiles. For the millionth time since our divorce, I was thankful we'd split amicably. This conversation would be a hell of a lot more awkward if we were already at odds.

After he'd ordered a drink, he folded his hands under his chin and rested his elbows on the table. "So, what's up? You said you needed to talk about something?"

"Yeah." I chewed my lip. "I..." Fuck, for all the time I'd spent playing out this conversation in my head, now I had no idea where to start.

His eyes widened slightly, and he cocked his head. "Is everything okay?"

"Yeah, yeah, everything's fine." I took a deep breath. "Listen, I've been seeing someone for the last few weeks. A couple of months, now, actually."

He smiled. "Good, I'm glad to hear it."

My smile wasn't as enthusiastic, and the furrow of his brow told me that hadn't escaped his noticed. I cleared my throat and went on. "He's a great guy, and things are going really well."

"Does he get along with the kids?"

"He hasn't met them," I said. "I'd like him to, though, and that's why we're here. I wanted to talk to you first."

"You don't have to ask me before you introduce someone to them, Jocelyn. You know that."

"There are some"—I paused, searching for the right words—"different circumstances."

He raised an eyebrow. "Different in what way?"

I wrapped both hands around my glass. "Like I said, he's a great guy. Really. But his job…" I trailed off, wondering where all the carefully rehearsed words had gone.

Michael gave a tentative laugh. "What is he? A hit man or a drug dealer or something?"

"Oh, God, no." I managed a laugh myself. "He's…" I chewed my lip. Finally, I took a deep breath and looked my ex-husband in the eye. "He's an escort."

Michael's brow furrowed. Then his eyebrows jumped. "Wait, an escort? Like, an *escort*?"

I nodded slowly.

He rubbed the bridge of his nose. "He's a prostitute. You're dating…a prostitute."

I let out my breath. "Yes."

"I'm not sure I want to know," he said, leaning back in his chair and looking at me, "but how the hell did you meet this guy?"

I looked at him. Didn't blink. Didn't say a word.

The upward flick of his eyebrow signaled his enlightenment. "Are you serious?"

"Yes. It's a long story."

"One I really don't want to hear." Disgust dripped from every word.

My stomach twisted itself into tighter knots. "Well, it happened. And now—"

"And quite frankly, I'm surprised." He scowled. "I never thought of you as that type."

"You try doing the single thing for seven years without a prospect in sight, and see what lengths you'll go to," I snapped.

He narrowed his eyes. "I can't say I'd ever go with a prostitute."

"I didn't think I would either." I shrugged, watching myself wring my hands on the table. "I was just tired of the headache and bullshit with dating and needed some—"

"Yeah." He put a hand up. "I get it. What I don't get is how you went from renting this guy to dating him. I mean..." He narrowed his eyes. "How many times did you use him, anyway?"

"A few."

"And how did you get from that to whatever it is you're doing now?"

I sighed. "We got to know each other."

With a sniff of sarcasm, he said, "I'll say you did."

"Michael, please."

He shifted in his chair and rested his elbows on the table. "So, what now? Are things, um, serious? I assume they are if we're having this conversation."

"They're getting that way, yes," I said quietly. "I don't want to get too far into it or start thinking about it being a permanent thing until he's met the kids. You've been there."

"Yes, but I wasn't seeing a prostitute."

I resisted the urge to reach across the table and throttle him. "He *is* a human being, you know."

"Mm-hmm." He raised an eyebrow, challenging me to break through the thick wall of preconceived notions.

Trying not to roll my eyes, I said, "I know it's unusual. It's—"

"Unusual? You're suggesting bringing someone like that around our kids."

"There's more to him than just his line of work, Michael," I threw back. "He wouldn't dream of telling the kids or breathing a word about it around them. He knows how to be discreet."

Michael snorted. "Oh, I'll bet he does."

I glared at him. "I'm serious. Just give him a chance."

"To what, Jocelyn?" He rubbed the bridge of his nose. "Someone like that isn't parent material. He's—"

"First of all, I'm not looking for a parent," I said. "I'm looking for a companion. Our kids *have* a father."

"You know what I mean." He eyed me. "Doesn't it bother you that he's still doing this while he's dating you?"

"I'm not crazy about it, but it *is* how he pays his bills."

"Has he thought about doing anything else?" He smirked. "Or is he happy in his line of work?"

"This from the man who knows how difficult it is to change careers with the way the economy is now?"

"So, what?" He drummed his fingers on the table beside his drink. "He's desperate? Struggling? 'Woe is me, I have to fuck other women for a living'?"

I refused to give him the satisfaction of a flinch. "Are you done? Because I'd like to have a serious conversation about this."

"Okay, I'm sorry." He folded his hands and shifted again. "You do understand why this is a bit, erm, hard to swallow, right?"

"Yes, I do." I exhaled. "Believe me, no one knows like I do how strange this is."

He regarded me silently for a long moment. When he spoke again, his tone was gentle. "Then why do you do it, Jocelyn?"

"Why do you think?" I asked, almost whispering.

"You really feel that strongly about him?"

I nodded. "I haven't had this kind of connection with someone in..." I shook my head. "In ages. Really, I don't think I've ever had something like this with anyone."

He stared into his drink but didn't speak.

Leaning forward, I said, "You know me, Michael. You know I would never put the kids in a dangerous situation or let someone around them who I didn't fully trust."

"I know." He ran a hand through his hair and released a breath. "I've never questioned your judgment when it comes to the kids."

"Except now," I said, and it wasn't a question.

With a sigh of resignation, he nodded. "I'm sorry, I can't just say this is fine and pretend it doesn't bother me."

"What would it take for you to be comfortable with it?"

He swallowed hard, lips tightening as if the very taste of that thought made him queasy. "Well, for starters, I at least want to meet this guy before the kids do."

"I figured you would. In fact..." I glanced at my watch. "He'll be here any minute."

"What?" Michael's eyes widened. "He's coming here? Now?"

"Yes."

"Gee, thanks for giving me time to get my head around the idea," he snarled.

"Look, I just want you to meet him and get it over with. He's probably nowhere near what you're expecting."

"We'll see about that," he muttered into his drink.

As if on cue, the bells above the door rang again, and our heads turned. My heart jumped, half because of the sight of Austin, half because of the conversation I was dreading.

Michael looked toward the door, then at me, and lowered his voice. "That's him, I assume?"

"That's him."

"I see." His tone was flat, betraying neither disgust nor surprise, but the hint of a growl underscored the hostility in his stiff posture. He watched Austin approach, and it was just as well I couldn't hear his thoughts. He watched my boyfriend like he was sizing up a rival, memorizing movements and guessing weak spots. Michael wasn't the violent type by any means, but he was as protective of our kids as I was, and this newcomer was, in his eyes, a threat.

And Austin saw it. Though his expression was mostly neutral, the tightness of his jaw and the narrowness of his eyes responded to Michael's unspoken assessment with a silent "is there a problem?"

Oh, Jesus. Please play nice. Both of you.

I gestured at Austin. "Michael, this is Austin. Austin, Michael."

Austin extended his hand, and Michael eyed it warily, wrinkling his nose just enough to give me the almost irresistible urge to kick him under the table.

"Don't worry," Austin said with a hint of a smirk. "I wash my hands between clients." That nearly prompted me to redirect that kick, but to my surprise, Michael's cheeks colored, and with a sheepish look, he shook Austin's hand.

"Nice to meet you," he said through gritted teeth.

"Likewise," Austin growled. He took a seat beside me and casually rested his arm across the back of my chair. My ex-husband had never shown a flicker of jealousy toward any guy I'd dated, but this time, I didn't miss the hint of tautness in his lips.

Well, *this* was off to a good start.

I opened my mouth to speak, but Michael beat me to it.

"I'll give you some credit," he said with a sneer. "You don't look like a prostitute."

Austin shrugged. "I don't usually wear the fishnets and garish makeup on my day off."

In spite of wanting to elbow him, I smothered a laugh. My ex-husband stared incredulously at Austin for a moment, then allowed himself a quiet chuckle.

"Touché." He straightened his posture and squared his shoulders. "Jocelyn's told me a few things about you."

"So I gathered," Austin said drily.

"Right." Michael played with his straw, absently stabbing at ice cubes. "Look, it sounds like the two of you are happy together. And I'm thrilled, honestly. But..." He trailed off.

I sighed. "Michael, we—"

"How exactly am I supposed to trust someone in your line of work around my kids?" Michael blurted out.

"What the fuck does my line of work have to do with kids?" Austin snapped, and the fury in his voice startled both my ex-husband and me.

Sitting back, Michael put his hands up. "Look, I'm not—"

"Save it," Austin snarled. "I've heard it all before from plenty of people. That's why I'm never alone with my nieces and nephews or anyone else's kids, because people assume that just because I'm a sex worker, I'm also a goddamned child molester."

At nearby tables, a few heads turned, and I wondered if it was "sex worker" or "child molester" that caught their attention.

Austin didn't seem to notice, but he did lower his voice. "Listen, my work involves sex with consenting adults. It has *nothing* to do with children. You can think what you want about me, judge me all you want for selling sex to adults who choose to buy it, but don't you *dare* insinuate I'd *ever* lay a hand on a child. Yours or anyone else's."

Michael stammered for a second, then collected himself. "I'm sure you can understand the sentiment of someone when it comes to the morals—"

"Yeah, I've heard it all," Austin said. "I'm sure you'd be fine with me if I was something respectable and honest, like a lawyer or a politician." With a smirk, he added, "Hey, at least my clients *know* I'm going to screw them."

Michael said nothing.

His voice gentler now, Austin said, "I know you want to protect your kids. I understand that, and I respect it. You have every right to feel safe with whoever your kids interact with. But don't rely on what society's told you about people like me."

"Besides the fact that you—"

"Yes, *besides* that," Austin growled.

"Okay, but even if I did find that palatable—and I don't," Michael said. "There's also the legal aspect of it. It *is* a criminal activity, is it not?"

Austin shrugged. "And depending on the state, so are anal sex, oral sex, and sex outside of marriage. It's a victimless crime between two adults."

"A victimless crime?" Michael raised an eyebrow. "What about the spouses of your clients?"

"Their spouses are the victims of adultery, not prostitution." Austin took his arm off my chair and folded his hands on the table. "I don't condone that aspect of it. Never have. But it's part and parcel with my occupation, so I live with it. The adultery is on her, though. Not me."

"Yes, I can tell you lose loads of sleep over it."

"I'll be sure to confess my sins when I get to hell." Austin narrowed his eyes. "I'm sure I'll be able to find a child-molesting priest or two to listen to me."

Michael scowled. "Okay, fine, it's illegal, and you have no problem with it. However, I have a problem with my children being exposed to it."

"Exposed to what?" Austin scoffed. "Do you think I'm going to tell them about it? What kind of—"

"Okay, okay, both of you." I put my hands up and shot each of them a glare. "We're not going to get anywhere like this. Can we *please* discuss this like civil adults?"

Both nodded. Michael took a breath and looked at Austin. "So, how would this work? I mean, what do you tell them you do for a living?"

"My usual cover story is that I'm an artist," he said. "I paint, and I also do graphic-design work. Which is true. I really do those things."

Michael raised an eyebrow. "And you're 'stuck' doing this job?"

"Michael," I growled.

"Sorry, sorry," he said.

"To answer your question," Austin said. "Yes, I am 'stuck' if I want a steady paycheck."

Michael pursed his lips. A few snide retorts were probably on the tip of his tongue, but he wisely let them go. Steepling his fingers in front of his lips and resting his elbows on the table, he said, "So the kids wouldn't know what you're really doing, then."

"Absolutely not," I said.

"I wouldn't discuss it with them," Austin said.

"Which brings me to another question," Michael said. "Hypothetically, let's say you're staying around for a while. Mikey is getting to the age where he's going to start getting...curious. Lex isn't far behind him, especially being as precocious as she is." He folded his hands under his chin. "So what happens if one of them comes to you with questions?"

"That depends on what you and Jocelyn are comfortable with me saying," Austin said. "I'm not going to start telling them war stories as examples, if that's what you're worried about."

Michael laughed. "No, I wasn't worried about that, I guess. But the thing is, they ask my wife questions sometimes. For whatever reason, sometimes they're more comfortable with her than with the two of us, and I trust her to give them correct information. Jocelyn and I have discussed it with her; she knows what we're comfortable with. And I..." He paused, taking a deep breath, and looked Austin in the eye. "I need to be able to trust you the same way."

Austin nodded. "I understand. Look, if one of your kids came to me and asked me something, I wouldn't overstep any bounds you two lay down. Yeah, I'm probably a bit more liberal than most when it comes to all things sexual, but you're the parents. If they came to me, I'd be as open with information as you two are comfortable." He paused. "I was a teenager once too, you know, so it's not like I wouldn't be able to empathize with them and not overwhelm or confuse them."

"I appreciate that," Michael said quietly. "Though I'm sure you can understand if I still have reservations about someone in your line of work being around my kids, let alone discussing things like that with them."

"You're missing the point here," Austin said. "They'd be around me, not my line of work. It's not who I am; it's just what I do for a living."

Michael's lips thinned. Before he could throw something counterproductive into the conversation, I broke in.

"Let me ask you this, Michael."

He looked at me, inclining his head slightly to bid me to continue.

I glanced at Austin, then turned to my ex-husband. "If you'd met Austin before I told you what he does for a living, would you have guessed? Just by talking to him? Looking at him?"

Michael chewed his lip. After a moment, he released a breath and shook his head. "No. No, I wouldn't have."

"And neither will the kids," I said. "Look, if I hadn't told you, you probably never would have known. The only reason I told you is because I think you deserve to know, and because I think you're reasonable enough to see him for who he is, not what he is."

He said nothing.

"Trust me," Austin said softly. "You're not the first to be weirded out by this, and I guarantee you won't be the last. But whatever I can do to show you I would sooner throw myself in front of a bus than harm your kids..."

"Well." Michael pulled back his sleeve to look at his watch, then glanced out the window. "I think the next bus should be here in—"

"*Michael*." I laughed, and so did they.

"All right, point taken." Michael looked at Austin. "Would you mind if I speak to Jocelyn alone for a minute? Won't be long, I promise."

"Sure, that's fine." Austin kissed me gently and stood. "I'll wait for you outside."

As soon as Austin was out of earshot, Michael looked at me. "So you two really are serious about this. About having him meet the kids and...well, whatever it is you're doing."

I nodded. "This isn't something we just jumped into and didn't think about. With his job, and with the kids, we knew it could get complicated."

Shaking his head slowly, he said, "I don't know how you do it. I really don't think I could deal with that."

"Well, I..." I shrugged, trailing off for a moment. "I just don't see him as anyone other than Austin. Now that I know him, what he does for a living is... irrelevant."

Michael said nothing.

"I know this is a really strange thing, and I know you want to protect the kids," I said. "But please, don't take them from me over this."

He jumped like I'd actually kicked him under the table as I'd been tempted to do a few times. "Jocelyn, I wouldn't do that. You know that." He glanced in Austin's direction. "This is just going to take some time to sink in. I promise I'm not going to take the kids from you, but will you hold off on introducing him to them for right now?"

Swallowing hard, I nodded. "If that's what you want, yeah."

"Thank you," he whispered. "I guess that's all we needed to discuss, then?"

"Yeah. I'm sorry it was a bit awkward..."

He poked at ice in his drink again. "I can't imagine a conversation like this not being awkward, to be honest."

"Good point." I dropped my gaze, but then made myself look at him. "Thank you, though."

He met my eyes and offered a halfhearted smile. "Thanks for talking to me about him before getting the kids involved."

"You know I'd never blindside you with something like this."

He laughed. "To be fair, I never thought you'd *do* something like this."

"That makes two of us."

His laughter faded a bit. "And yes, it's a little weird, but..." He glanced in Austin's direction again and exhaled. "You guys really are happy together, aren't you?"

"Yeah, we are." It was my turn to glance at Austin. "It's been strange. I won't lie. But he's a great guy."

Michael nodded slowly and took a breath. "Well, occupation notwithstanding, it's good to see you happy with someone. It's been way too long."

"Tell me about it."

He looked at his watch again. "I should run. Carrie and the kids are waiting on me."

"Right. Okay."

We both stood and went to the counter to take care of our tabs. Once we'd paid, we went outside to join Austin.

"It was, um, nice meeting you, Austin," Michael said. "Even if we got off to a rocky start."

"It happens," Austin said. "And it was nice meeting you too."

"All things considered right?" Michael laughed.

"Yeah." Austin chuckled. "All things considered."

My ex-husband looked at his watch. "Well, I'd better go." He hugged me and kissed my cheek. Then he and Austin exchanged a handshake that was far less hostile than their initial one.

Michael started down the sidewalk, and we headed in the opposite direction. Austin slipped his hand into mine.

"Well, that was relatively painless," he said.

"Better than I expected it to be." I shot him a playful glare. "Though was it *really* necessary to antagonize him?"

Austin didn't even try to look sheepish. "He started it."

Rolling my eyes, I elbowed him. "Jesus, do I have to keep the two of you separated?"

"Wouldn't break my heart," he said.

"I'm sure."

Austin laughed, then released my hand and put his arm around my waist. "He really wasn't that bad. Trust me, I expected a lot worse."

"Still," I said. "I wanted to smack him about half a dozen times."

"Yeah, me too." He smiled. "Honestly, it's okay. I'm just glad he didn't get too bent out of shape or threaten to take your kids."

I shook my head. "No, he won't. He told me as much, and I trust him."

Austin nodded. "Good."

I chewed my lip. "He *would* like us to hold off on having you meet the kids, though." I looked up at him. "Are you, I mean, I hope that's—"

"Jocelyn." Austin stopped, and so did I. He touched my face and looked in my eyes. "Baby, of course I'm okay with it. There's no rush for any of this. If he needs some time, that's fine."

"I know. It just bugs me when people treat you like a damned leper."

Austin laughed softly. "It could be a lot worse, believe me." He kissed my forehead. "Today was a good start, and he'll come around. Besides," he said, combing his fingers through my hair, "I'm not going anywhere."

"Actually, yes you are."

His eyes widened. "I...am?"

"Mm-hmm." I grinned, sliding my hands up the front of his shirt. "You're going back to my place. With me."

One corner of his mouth rose slightly. "And what am I going to do when I get there?"

"Don't know." I grasped his shirt and pulled him closer to me. "You tell me."

Chapter Sixteen

Austin's schedule was tricky to plan around, mostly owing to the fact that there *was* no schedule. He had set days during the week when he'd turn off his work phone and be unavailable, but on the days when that phone was on, it was anyone's guess when it would ring. When it did, the resulting client session could be days away or, as he'd warned me up front, within hours.

That meant, of course, there were times when he had to cancel some plans with me at the last minute to go to work.

Go to work. That was such a benign way to phrase it. Anyone would think I meant he was dropping into the office for some overtime, or going in to get a network back online, or seeing a client in the more socially acceptable sense of the phrase. Something other than apologizing profusely, kissing me good-bye, and leaving to go fuck another woman.

Every time he did, I talked myself into believing it didn't bother me, but lately, I'd had a hard time convincing myself of that. Each time that phone rang, it wore me down a little more, and when it rang tonight, whether I wanted to admit it or not, it bothered me. A lot.

I hadn't said a word to him about it. I wanted to believe I could get over it. I wanted to believe that as much as I wanted to believe what we had was more than just a desperate need to cling to someone who didn't see me as damaged goods. Was I sticking around because I really wanted to be with Austin, or because I was afraid no one else would want to be with me?

Fuck, I'm going to drive myself insane.

If I thought about it enough, I was sure I *would* drive myself insane, so as soon as his car had pulled out of my driveway, I focused my energy on finding the nearest available way to *not* think about where he'd gone. Some company and some alcohol seemed like a good distraction, so I called Janie. She was out with her other half, though, so I tried Kim to see if she minded me tagging along at the last minute. Of course she didn't mind. She was always game for more company. That, and we hadn't seen each other in quite some time. We'd e-mailed, but as far as getting together, she'd been busy and, well, since I'd met Austin, so had I.

"Absolutely!" she'd practically squealed into the phone. "Long time no see, so it'll be good to hang out." Her other two friends, Jackie and Tina, would be joining her at a velvet-rope nightclub downtown, so she promised to save me a seat and have a mojito waiting for me.

Little black dress, dab of makeup, and I was on my way.

Two things didn't occur to me until the cab had dropped me off, I'd paid the cover, and Kim had already spotted me from across the room.

One, she was the one who'd referred me to Elite Escorts in the first place.

Two, the woman didn't have a discreet bone in her body.

"Hey, you," she said when I took a seat beside her at their booth. As promised, my mojito awaited, but before I'd even taken a deliciously alcoholic swallow, Kim said, "So did you ever take my advice?"

I forced myself not to choke on my drink. "What?"

"You know what I'm talking about." She elbowed me. "Did you call the agency?"

Across the table, Jackie's eyes lit up. "Oh? You're getting in on them too?"

"Another member of the club," Tina said. "Welcome to the Elite Escort connoisseurs."

Oh. Fuck.

I took another drink, then cleared my throat. "Well, I...um..."

"Come on," Kim said. "Spill it. I want to know." She smirked like she could see right through me. "You haven't complained about bad sex or no sex in your e-mails recently, so I'm guessing either you called or you've found a man. Which is it?"

How about both?

My cheeks betrayed me. With the heat beneath my skin, there was no way my complexion had remained an unincriminating shade, especially not when Kim squealed and grabbed my hand.

"Ooh! You did! So how was it? Who'd you get?"

My eyes darted toward other girls at the table, and they had the same "you did, didn't you?" expressions.

Jackie grinned over her cosmopolitan. "Yeah, come on, tell us."

"Wait," I said. "You've all really used Elite Escorts? Seriously?"

"Of course we have." Jackie clicked her tongue. "Sweetie, we work as many hours as you do, and dating's a pain in the ass."

"Amen," Tina said. "I'll be forty in two weeks. I may not be able to find a man who's worth keeping, but at least I'm still getting some."

I stared into my mojito. Couldn't imagine why these three were all single. But then, so was I, at least until recently. Until I'd resorted to it out of desperation, which became a habit, which oddly enough resulted in a relationship, which was exactly why I was here tonight, which—

I downed the second half of my drink in one swallow.

"So, give us details," Kim said.

"Oh, um, it was..." I paused, clearing my throat. "It was worth the money."

All three of them laughed.

"With those boys, I don't think it's possible for it not to be worth the money," Kim said.

"I'll drink to that," Jackie said.

"Me too." Tina paused. "Well, at least now that Mario is gone."

Kim wrinkled her nose. "Oh, God, he was a dud."

"Never used him," Jackie said.

"You're lucky," Tina muttered. "One and only time I ever asked for my money back."

I raised my eyebrows. "Okay, I'm curious. How often *do* you all use the agency?"

"Every time I get an alimony check." Tina grinned and raised her glass in a mock salute. "Dale decided to cheat, so now he's paying for me to get some action."

And here I'd felt like an addict for my four paid sessions with Sabian.

"Must be nice," Jackie said. "Ever since I moved into the new condo, my play money has pretty much dried up."

"Had to settle for dating normal guys, then?" Kim asked.

Jackie rolled her eyes and nodded. "Unfortunately." With a wistful sigh, she added, "I miss my boy toys."

My stomach turned. This was a mistake. Of all the places I could have gone tonight to forget what my boyfriend did for a living, I'd plunked myself right in the middle of three regular customers for Elite Escorts. Oh, God, what if one of them had been with Sabian?

I shuddered and flagged down the cocktail waitress for an emergency mojito.

Oh, but the girls weren't done yet.

"So, who did you get?" Kim asked me. "You still haven't told us."

"I, um." I gulped, glancing around for the nearest exit. "I don't remember his name, to be honest."

"You don't remember?" Tracy snickered. "He didn't make much of an impression, then?"

He made an impression, all right. "I, well, it's been a while now. A few weeks. I just can't remember his name."

"Well, what did he look like?" Jackie asked. "Obviously he was hot, ripped, and well-endowed, or he wasn't with Elite Escorts." All three of them laughed, and my stomach turned. They saw this as some kind of female bonding thing, a dirty little secret we all shared, something to giggle over like schoolgirls. Maybe it would have been if things hadn't turned out the way they had with Austin, but now this was a conversation I just couldn't stomach.

Coming out here tonight was definitely not a good idea. I needed my drink. Or a quick escape. Or both. A mojito to go.

Kim elbowed me again. "Come on, come on, spill it, woman."

"Oh, um, he was…" I cleared my throat. "Definitely hot."

"Definitely wasn't Max, then." Kim laughed. "You'd remember him, believe me. Hot doesn't even begin to describe him. That man is the living definition of the Italian stallion. *Rawr.*"

"Or Curtis. He is, and will always be, my favorite." Tracy fanned herself. "The things he can do with his mouth, Lord have mercy."

Kim laughed. "You *obviously* haven't spent enough time with Sabian then."

My mouth went dry, and my throat closed around my breath. The waitress was a saint, because she arrived right then with my drink. While I tried to drown myself in the alcohol, my companions went on.

"Oh, Sabian's good with his mouth," Jackie said with all the matter-of-factness of someone who had no clue she was talking about someone else's boyfriend. *Oh, God, this is too weird for words.* "But nowhere near as good as Xander."

"No no no." Kim shook her head and gestured with her drink. "Xander's good, I'll give you that. But Sabian? He could give lessons on eating pussy."

I swallowed the bile rising in my throat.

"Well, to each her own," Jackie said. "And even if he's not as good as Xander with his mouth, Sabian's got them all beat with what he's got in his pants."

I'm going to be sick. Any second. I'm going to be sick.

"He certainly lasts longer than most," Tina said. "Though Daren gives him a run for his money."

"God, yes, he does." Kim whistled. "He has to be on something, I swear it. No man has endurance like that without taking something."

Jackie grinned and picked up her drink. "He can take whatever he wants, as long as he keeps doing what he does."

"I thought Heath and Sabian were both taking pills," Tina said. "But no way. They can both practically come on command. No way a guy on Viagra can do that."

Stop. Stop. Please. All of you. Just shut up.

God, how did I end up in this twilight zone? At a table with three women who'd had sex with my boyfriend. Listening to them compare notes. While he was out. While he was out with a client doing God only knew what while I tried to drown in a drink.

Right this second, he could be going down on her. Or fucking her. Or—

I "accidentally" bumped my mostly full glass, tipping it into my lap. "Oh, shit!" I flew upright, brushing ice and mint leaves off my skirt. "I'd better go clean this up. I'll, um, be right back." I grabbed my purse off the bench and barely kept myself from sprinting across the club to the restroom.

Since it was early yet and the crowd was still light, the restroom was mercifully empty. I pulled a few paper towels from the dispenser and pretended not to notice the way my hands shook while I cleaned off my clothes. Sponging off my dress with a wadded paper towel gave me something to do, at least. Something besides grabbing on to the sink and staring into my own reflection, demanding answers to the millions of questions running through my brain. That or darting into one of the stalls to heave a few times.

I thought I was okay with this. I thought I could handle being with an escort. *Jesus, who are you kidding, Jocelyn? An escort? He's a prostitute. A gigolo. A whore.* The man sold sex like I sold advertising deals. And I was fooling myself into believing I could deal with sharing him with anyone with the cash to pay his price.

What was I thinking?

The restroom door opened, letting some of the thumping music from the club spill in before it shut with a dull thud and cut off the noise. Stiletto heels clunked on the tile floor.

"You okay, hon?" Kim asked.

No. No, I'm not okay. My boyfriend's...out there. Somewhere. He's...goddammit, he's fucked you. And Jackie. And Tina.

I clenched my jaw to keep the rising nausea at bay. "I'm fine."

"You sure? You look pale as hell."

I glanced in the mirror. It just figured a place like this was posh enough to have warm, incandescent lighting in the bathrooms instead of harsh fluorescents. At least the latter would have been an easy scapegoat for my pallor.

"I'm, I guess, just not used to everyone being so...candid." I swallowed. "About their sex lives."

Kim cocked her head. "But we always talk like that."

"Right. Right." I shifted my weight. "But it's different now for some reason. I don't know exactly why." *Liar, liar, booze-drenched skirt on fire.*

"Probably a little weird realizing we've all fished from the same pond, I guess."

That didn't help my nausea. At all. "Something like that," I muttered.

"Honestly, hon, it's not that big of a deal."

I took a deep breath. It was a big deal. Jesus, if she had a clue.

Fuck it, if anyone in my world wouldn't be judgmental of my choice in men, it would be her. Michael was quite a bit more conservative than Kim, after all, particularly when it came to all things sexual, and even he hadn't taken it as badly as I'd thought he would. Kim, sexually liberated as she was, stood a good chance of being at least somewhat receptive to my unorthodox situation. Someone who partook in this kind of thing was obviously open-minded enough to view it as something reasonably acceptable. On one hand, the men of Elite Escorts were precisely what she demanded in a man. Well-groomed, well-dressed, and at least in the case of the one I'd been with nearly every night this week, well-hung. On the other, they *were* escorts. Considering this was a woman who didn't think a man was relationship material unless he owned a yacht, she could see Austin as a hell of a prize or a complete slimeball.

"Can I be completely honest about something?" I asked.

"Sure, yeah." She rested her hip against the counter. The humor faded from her heavily made-up face. "Is everything okay?" Her eyes widened. "Did something bad happen with one of the guys? Oh my God, hon, I'd feel horrible. Tell me—"

"No, nothing happened." I paused. "Nothing bad."

Her brightly painted lips twisted into a smirk. "Haven't been able to find anything better? It's easy to get spoiled with these guys. Believe me." She winked. "I know."

"Something like that." I blew out a breath. "So, I'm guessing you're pretty familiar with Sabian?"

Her eyes lit up. "Am I familiar with him?" She fanned herself. "Oh, am I. He's—"

I put a hand up and shook my head. "Okay, okay, I don't want details."

"You don't, but I do." She grinned. "Do tell."

"Um, well, I've seen him a few times, actually."

"Can't blame you there."

I glared at her.

"Okay, so what's wrong?" she asked.

"The thing is, I'm…seeing him." I swallowed. "Like, regularly."

"My God, you've got him on a schedule or something?" She laughed. "No wonder he hasn't been available much lately."

I cringed. This was par for the course dating someone in his line of work, but I'd be the first to admit it was weird as hell. Avoiding her eyes, I said, "No, I mean I'm seeing him." I looked at her, bracing for her reaction.

"Seeing him?" She cocked her head. Then her eyebrows shot up. "You mean, like, *dating* him?"

I nodded slowly.

She rubbed her forehead, then blinked a few times. "You're dating him? Him? *Sabian?*"

I took a deep breath. "Yes, I am."

"But he's…" She shook her head. "He's…he's a…"

"A prostitute?"

"Yes. *That.*" Disgust oozed from that single word, and I knew this conversation was as much a mistake as coming to the club in the first place tonight.

"I know he is," I said quietly. "Believe me, I know."

"And it doesn't bother you?"

Oh, it does. I shrugged. "It's…different."

"Different?" She snorted. "He's a *whore*, Jocelyn."

Folding my arms across my chest, I said, "And?"

"And?" She laughed and rolled her eyes. "You really don't see the problem here?"

"I'm not going to lie and say it isn't weird." I shrugged. "But he's a great guy, Kim."

"Sure, I guess," she said with a sneer. "If you discount all of the places he gets paid to put his dick."

I tried not to visibly cringe. "Please, Kim, don't act like you think it's dirty. You've been with him too." *Christ, I really am living in a damned twilight zone.*

"Yeah, I have," she said. "He's worth a roll in the hay for a few hundred bucks, but relationship material? No way."

"Why not? Because he isn't a damned billionaire?"

"No, because he's a whore." She huffed and rolled her eyes again. "Look, a guy dating a hooker? That's amusing. Amusing, pathetic, and so *obviously* just for sex and arm candy, it's—" She cut herself off and gestured sharply. "For heaven's sake, you're a mother. Are you going to introduce this guy to your kids?"

"Not at the moment, no," I said through gritted teeth. "But Michael knows about him. And he knows what he does for a living."

She wrinkled her nose. "And he's on board with that? It doesn't bother him at all what you'd be exposing his children to?"

"Do you *hear* yourself?" I said. "Austin's not a piece of meat. He doesn't advertise what he does, he—"

"Which should give you a clue right there," she said. "If it's not such a big deal, why doesn't he tell people?"

"Oh, I don't know." I rolled my eyes. "Maybe because of the preconceived notions and assumptions people have about him?"

"Like the fact that he has sex with other women for money?" She laughed humorlessly. "That's not a preconceived notion; that's his job description."

"That's all it is," I said. "There's more to him than his job, you know."

"Jocelyn." She raised a pencil-thin eyebrow. "He has sex. With other women. For a living. Hell, I've been with him. More than once."

I forced back the growing queasiness. "Look, I know it's unusual. It's been weird as hell for me to adjust to it, but him being an escort doesn't change what we're like together."

"Except he's selling what he gives you. Not exactly special, is it?"

"Does it have to be? It's sex." I leaned against the counter and folded my arms across my chest. "That, and having sex for money doesn't mean he has what *we* have with anyone else."

"How do you know he doesn't?" She cocked her head and raised both eyebrows. "He's obviously managed to have what the two of you have with *one* of his clients. What's to stop him from having it with another?"

I didn't know how to answer that. Deep down, as much as I didn't want to admit it, I wondered the same thing.

"Think about it," she went on. "You think you've got something so special with him, but I could get on the phone right now, make an appointment, and go have sex with him. I could go fuck your man, Jocelyn, and you're telling me that doesn't bother you at all?"

I suppressed a shudder. "Yes. It does. Okay? Trust me, this hasn't been an easy thing to get used to. But he's—"

"Oh, Jesus." Another roll of the eyes. "He's. A. *Whore.* You're dating a *prostitute.* Someone who sells his body to any woman who wants it and doesn't bat an eye."

I set my jaw. "So tell me, why is it okay for you to pay him for sex, but when he wants to have a relationship with someone, it's suddenly disgusting?"

"Oh, he can have all the relationships he wants," she said. "What I can't figure out is why *you* have to scrape the bottom of the barrel and date someone like *that.*"

"Do you know anything about him, Kim?" I dug my fingers into my arms, barely resisting the urge to backhand her across the face. "Besides the fact that he's an escort?"

She gave a snort of laughter. "Oh, I know quite a bit about him. Probably some of the same things you do."

I narrowed my eyes. "I meant about *him.* As a person."

"No, I don't know a damned thing about him, and quite frankly, I don't care to." She sneered. "I don't need people like that in my life."

I released a sharp breath. "So that defines him, then? That's all he is, and all he'll ever be."

"Pretty much."

Narrowing my eyes, I said, "So if I told you I worked my way through two years of college as a lap dancer, you'd suddenly redefine me?"

She made a choked sound and her eyes widened. "You...did?"

"Does it change the way you look at me?"

Kim shifted her weight, and the disgusted down-up look she gave me hurt more than anything she'd said all evening. "Yeah, I'm not going to lie. It does."

I pursed my lips and rested my hands on the edge of the counter, tapping the marble slab with my nails. "I was never a lap dancer. I was just making a point. Even if I had been, you didn't know until this very moment, so that shouldn't negate all the years you have known me."

"And all I know of your little boy toy is that he's a whore." She shrugged so flippantly I wanted to smack her. "Quite frankly, I don't want to know anything else about him, because I don't want to associate with someone like that."

"Unless you're desperate and feel like a switch from your vibrator?"

"He puts himself out there as a piece of meat," she said. "So don't get all high and mighty with me for calling him what he is."

"And when he's not working? When he's just doing what normal people do?"

She shrugged again, and her smirk made my blood boil. "A piece of meat is still a piece of meat whether it's on my plate or in the freezer waiting to be cooked."

"Jesus Christ, Kim," I said, rolling my eyes. "Quit getting all high and mighty. It's not like you have any problem buying the commodity he's selling." I narrowed my eyes. "Tell me, would you get involved with a guy who'd used call girls as often as you've used escorts?"

She stiffened almost imperceptibly. "Depends."

"On?"

She shifted her weight. "On if he still used them, for one thing."

"And you'd be pissed as hell if he judged you for using Elite Escorts, wouldn't you?" I glared at her. "Or would you be too busy counting all the presents he's given you to see if it adds up to enough to buy sex with *you*?"

Kim's jaw dropped. "What?"

"You think it's different?" I folded my arms across my chest. "Deciding whether or not to put out based on his net worth, or the things he gives you? How is that any—"

"I am *not* a whore," she snarled.

"Aren't you?" I cocked my head. "So if a guy came along with not a lot of money and couldn't take you to five-star restaurants, you'd still consider him relationship material? Or if he didn't give you the jewelry you wanted or fly you to Jamaica, would you still fuck him?"

She glared at me. "That doesn't mean he's paying me for sex."

"Then what does it mean, Kim? Where's the line?" I took a breath. "Just because he doesn't give you cash doesn't mean it's not what you're doing."

Her lips twitched with the threat of a snarl. I braced myself, knowing what kind of screaming tirades this woman could unleash.

She didn't let fly, though. Instead, she spun on her heel and stormed out of the bathroom. When the slamming door cut off the thunder of angry stiletto-heeled footsteps, I exhaled and looked at myself in the mirror.

I didn't bother going back to the table. It wasn't at all like me to stick someone else with my tab, but I didn't feel too guilty about it this time. I'd just learned a hell of a lot more about my "friend" than I was ever comfortable knowing, and didn't feel the need to learn any more. By now, Jackie and Tina were probably in on it, and I didn't need to be outnumbered in this conversation.

Outside, I hailed a cab, gave the driver my address, and didn't even glance back to watch the club fade behind me. It wasn't the mojito and a half that had my stomach twisted in on itself. I spent the entire ride home with my fingers pressed against the bridge of my nose while I took long, deep breaths, willing myself not to find a reason—such as the pungent cab smell—to get sick.

Somehow I made it, and once I was home, I went into the living room and dropped onto the couch.

I thought about deleting Kim's number from my phone. I doubted she'd be calling, not after I'd confessed to dating a prostitute *and* called her a whore. There wouldn't be any outgoing calls in her direction either; life was too short to spend around people like that. Good riddance, if I was honest with myself. Kim and I had been friends for a long time, but she'd shown herself to be even shallower than I'd ever realized. If she could define someone like Austin that way, then I didn't need her in my life. There was a time when I'd thought along the same lines, but those days were gone. I couldn't go back. No matter how much Kim or anyone else turned up their noses at him, Austin was human.

I was also human. Only human. I had my limits, and while I didn't judge Austin for what he did, could I really be in a relationship with him?

Exhaling hard, I rubbed my forehead.

I couldn't do this. There was just no way. I was simply not wired to be the lover, girlfriend, whatever, to someone in Austin's line of work.

If I miss having sex with him, I thought bitterly, *I could always go buy an hour or two.*

My own thought made me flinch. But had I really thought I could do this? Really?

Maybe, deep down, I'd seen this as a challenge. Dating a sex worker was something another woman couldn't handle, but Jocelyn fucking Rhodes could do it without batting an eye. I didn't back down from any challenge. Ever. So was it the fear of admitting this was too much for me that had me all tied up in knots?

Or did I really not want to let him go?

Whatever it was, I had to call this off. I didn't want to hurt him, I didn't want to lose him, but I just couldn't do this.

Chapter Seventeen

The sick feeling in my gut refused to subside until Austin showed up the next evening. Though I was no longer worried about throwing up at the drop of a hat, now I had to contend with the ache in my throat that warned of impending tears. Guilt, confusion, and frustration all ganged up on me and threatened to show themselves if I let my guard down for even a second.

We couldn't do this. It had to stop. The closer I came to finding an opportunity to end it, though, the more it hurt to even consider. I had to let him go, but I didn't want to. Needed to. Couldn't.

Come on, Jocelyn. You have to. You're only fooling yourself if you think this can go anywhere. Or that it should *go anywhere.*

I glanced at Austin and realized he was looking at me. Probably had been for a long time. How long had I been lost in my own thoughts?

We were in my kitchen, a pot of coffee in my hand and two empty cups on the island in front of me.

From across the island, he cocked his head. "You okay, babe? You kind of spaced out."

"Yeah, I'm fine." I forced a smile. "Just zoning out. I guess."

His eyes narrowed just enough to suggest he saw right through me. "You've been quiet since I got here, and every time I touch you, you shrink away. Have I done something wrong?"

I set the coffeepot down and exhaled. Closing my eyes, I rubbed my forehead, willing myself to keep my emotions together. I silently begged him not to come closer, knowing full well he would. My senses followed his soft footsteps around the island, and when gentle hands squeezed my shoulders, the ache in my throat intensified.

"You sure you're okay?"

I nodded and sniffed sharply, refusing to let the tears make it past my eyes. "I'm sorry. I..."

His hands moved to my waist, and his lips against my cheek crumbled my defenses. I covered my eyes when a few hot tears escaped and slid down my face.

He wrapped his arms around me and kissed the side of my neck. "Baby, what's wrong?"

I quickly cleared my throat and collected my composure, but the damage was done. I couldn't pretend there was nothing on my mind. Not when he urged me to turn around and, when I faced him, brushed a tear from my cheek.

"Is this about last night?" he asked.

Another set of defenses fell. I avoided his eyes and let out a resigned breath. Then I nodded. Austin pulled me close to him. Stroking my hair, he kissed the top of my head, and damn it, why did it have to feel so damned good in his arms like this?

"I'm guessing it's not just because I had to change plans at the last minute."

"No. It's not." I fought back the threat of fresh tears. "I don't know if I can keep doing this, Austin."

He loosened his embrace, pulling back so we could see each other. Maybe giving me some comfortable distance too. Some breathing room.

I took a breath. "I thought I was okay with it. I did. But it's... I..."

"But it's bothering you more than you thought it would." It wasn't a question.

Sighing, I nodded slowly. "I'm sorry. It's..." I sniffed again and forced myself to look at him. "Austin, you've literally slept with three of my friends."

He blinked. "I have?"

"Yes." I sighed. "Well, former friends anyway. Once I told her about you..."

"You *told* her about me?" His eyes widened.

"I thought, if anyone would, she might understand." I shook my head. "But she just sees you and all the other escorts as pieces of meat."

He set his jaw.

"She's the one who referred me to the agency in the first place," I went on, "and while I was out with her and some friends last night, all of whom are regular customers, I got to listen to them comparing notes." I swallowed. "About you."

Austin dropped his gaze. He rubbed the back of his neck and let out a breath. "I'm sorry you had to listen to that."

"I guess it's par for the course." I tucked my hair behind my ear. "Part of dating an escort, I guess."

"Yeah, I guess it is."

"I'd love to say I can handle this." I ran a hand through my hair. "And I do want to make it work, but I'm not sure *how*."

"We make it work the same way anyone else makes a relationship work," he said. "The only difference is what I do for a living."

I raised an eyebrow. "That's a pretty sizeable difference, wouldn't you say?"

"Yes, it is," he said. "But there's more to us than that. There's more to me than that."

"I know there is." I exhaled. "I spent forever trying to explain that to someone last night. And on paper, it's so easy for me to say I can do this, and I want to do this, and..." I shook my head again, forcing back a flood of emotion. "But then I catch myself thinking about you while you're working, wondering who you're with, and what you're doing, and—"

"Baby, please." He smoothed my hair. "I know it's easier said than done, but don't let your imagination run off with you while I'm working. I—"

"It doesn't have to run very far, Austin," I said. "I *know* what it's like to be one of your clients."

He flinched. "Okay, I understand that. Really, I do. But I've told you, when I'm working, it's just business. It's a job. All physical, nothing emotional."

"*Most* of the time."

He said nothing.

I chewed my lip. "What do you—" I hesitated. Did I really want to know?

Austin put a hand on my waist. "What?"

"When you're, you know, working..." I paused, moistening my lips and silently berating myself for sounding like an awkward school kid. "What do you think about?"

He jumped, lips parting slightly like the question had caught him off guard. "You...really want to know?"

I nodded.

He took a breath. "I think about what I'm doing. How she's responding. What I need to do to keep her happy and make sure she gets her money's worth." He met my eyes. "It's so mechanical and businesslike, it's not even funny."

"Seriously?"

"Seriously." He gave me a playful grin. "What did you think I thought about?"

I shrugged, dropping my gaze again. "I don't know. I really don't. I guess, I mean I've had casual sex before, so it's not like I can't imagine having sex without an emotional connection, but I've never..." I trailed off, completely at a loss for how to finish the thought without it coming across as an accusation.

Austin lifted my chin. "You've never what?" He caressed my face. When the words I sought still didn't come, he said, "Look, I know this is weird for you, so if something's bothering you, even if you think it sounds stupid or petty, you can tell me."

I swallowed hard. Avoiding his eyes, I whispered, "I've never had emotionless sex with someone while I had an emotional connection with someone else." Just hearing myself say it made my stomach turn. I rubbed the bridge of my nose. "God, I don't even know what I'm saying, Austin. I'm... Fuck..."

"If you're worried I make a habit of this," he whispered, "don't be. I've never gotten involved with another client."

"But how do I know it won't happen?"

"You could just as easily get involved with one of your clients. It happens every damned day in the 'respectable' work world."

"I'm not having sex with my clients."

"And I'm *just* having sex with them," he said. "It's just sex. Babe, you can see the difference between that first time together and the way it is now, can't you? The sex is different. Everything is different." He paused, swallowing. "It wasn't the sex that did this, Jocelyn. It was everything in between."

I wanted to believe him, but Kim's words had burrowed their way into my uncertain consciousness.

"He's obviously managed to have what the two of you have with one of his clients. What's to stop him from having it with another?"

What *was* to stop him?

"Do you trust me?" he asked suddenly.

My head snapped up. "Yes, of course I do. Or we wouldn't have gotten this far."

He stroked my hair. "Then trust me, babe."

I sighed. "I want to, Austin. Everything about this is just so... It's..."

"I know." He kissed my forehead. "I know this isn't easy for you. The thing is..." He trailed off. Took a breath. Looked me in the eye. "Babe, whatever this is we're doing, this kind of thing doesn't happen every day. Regardless of what anyone involved does for a living. That, and you're the first woman in I don't know how long who's seen me as something other than a whore."

"That's...part of the problem."

"What do you mean?"

"I can see past your job like other women can't or won't," I said. "Just like you can see past the fact that I'm a single mom the way very few men seem willing to." I chewed my lip. "But is that all this is?"

"Do..." He paused, furrowing his brow. "Do you really think that's all this is?"

I dropped my gaze. "I don't know what I think. I'm just afraid this is...that I'm kidding myself." I met his eyes. "Are we both kidding ourselves? We've both had such a hard time finding someone who could see past what we are, and I want to believe we're in this because of who we are. Not...not just because we don't see each other as damaged goods."

He blinked. "What are you saying?"

I took a deep breath. "I'm saying I'm scared we're doing this because we're afraid no one else will."

Austin flinched. He took a step back and leaned against the opposite counter, drumming his fingers on the granite. For a long moment, he didn't speak, and he didn't look at me. I was afraid he'd be angry, but when his eyes finally rose to meet mine, he looked hurt more than anything.

"Listen, a lot of people say a lot of things about me and what I do," he said softly. "I can deal with it when people call me a cheap whore, a hooker, a piece of meat, whatever." Though I couldn't be sure, I thought his voice threatened to crack when he added, "But don't call me insincere."

"I didn't mean it like that," I said. "What I—"

"Jocelyn, I don't expect this to be easy for you. Not in the least." He took a deep breath. "But this, what we're doing—I don't know what I can do to convince you it's real."

I avoided his eyes.

"The fact that you can accept me for what I am," he said, "that just opened the door. Everything else? That happened on its own. And quite honestly, I don't care if another woman would take me and all the crap that comes with me, because she wouldn't be you, so it wouldn't matter."

I swallowed the lump in my throat. Austin came back toward me and touched my face.

"Baby, I can't change what I am," he said. "Even if I found another job tomorrow and never needed another penny from the agency again, I'll always be a man who has sold sex for a living."

I winced.

"Listen to me," he said. "I don't underestimate for a second how weird this is for you. It took a strong woman to even consider giving this a try, and it's a lot harder in practice than it is on paper. If it's..." He paused, swallowing hard. Even softer now, he said, "If it's not something you can handle, I'll understand."

My heart flipped. He was giving me an out. A chance to walk away with no hard feelings and no resentment.

"It's up to you," he said, caressing my face as he spoke. "If you want some time to think about it or if you want me to bow out now. Whatever you want to do, I'll understand either way."

My heart pounded. I'd had myself almost convinced that it was time to walk away, throw in the towel, call it quits. But he just had to go and say all the right things, and hold me like this, and give me an easy escape that was too damned hard to take. I wasn't sure how much of this relationship my sanity could take, but damn if I could convince myself, looking up at him now, that it wouldn't be worth a try.

I held his gaze. "What do *you* want to do?"

"I want to keep doing what we're doing," he said. "But not if it's going to be so stressful for you that it makes you miserable. I want you to be happy."

Shifting my weight, I forced myself to maintain eye contact, no matter how much I wanted to look anywhere but right at him. "You understand this is still an adjustment for me, right?"

"Of course." He kissed me gently. "We'll just take things a day at a time, just like we've done so far. If something's bothering you, don't hesitate to tell me. I want to know." He paused. "I may not always be able to fix it. I mean, this job has its...requirements. But don't keep it from me if it's bothering you."

"I won't."

"And if you need some time, just tell me," he whispered. "I don't think anyone could get their head around this overnight." He smoothed my hair. "Just remember one thing: regardless of how anyone chooses to define what I do for a living, I'm not selling what I'm giving you. If this isn't something you can handle, I'll understand, but I swear to you, I've never given this to anyone. I wouldn't dream of selling it, even if I could." He kissed me again, just barely letting his lips brush mine. "Just tell me if you need to let this go."

"Austin, I can't..." I closed my eyes, unable to look at him while I tried to gather my composure and struggled to pick a direction. Finally, I looked up at him and just let the words come on their own.

"I can't walk away from this."

"Are you sure?" He stroked my hair. "If you think it'll hurt or cause you more stress than it's worth—"

"I don't care right now."

"You tell me, then," he whispered. "What do you want me to do?"

My voice shook as badly as his hands and my knees when I said, "I want you to kiss me."

Austin grabbed me and kissed me, throwing both of us off balance and pulling the air right out of me. He gripped my hair like I gripped the back of his neck, and we stumbled until my back hit the counter.

"Baby, I want you so bad," he whispered between kisses. "Fuck, I..."

"Upstairs," was all I could say.

In a tangle of limbs and deep, passionate kisses, we stumbled out of the kitchen. All the way up the stairs and down the hall, we threw off clothes, kissed, touched, and how the hell had I fooled myself into thinking this was anything but real? And *right*? It had to be real. There was nothing fake about the way he kissed me or the way I had to force myself not to drag him down to the floor like I'd done one night not long ago. The way his hands gravitated to my face instead of my breasts or anywhere else was anything but fake, anything but wrong.

He managed to flip the light switch when we got into the bedroom, illuminating the room just before we fell into bed together. As soon as my back hit the mattress, he was over me, kissing me just as hungrily as he had all the way up the stairs.

Forget foreplay. Forget teasing each other. Forget anything other than getting as close as two people could possibly get.

We both sat up and went for the nightstand drawer, and between the two of us, we got the drawer open and one of those familiar gold foil squares out. Austin put the condom on as quickly as his trembling hands would allow, and as soon as it was in place, he threw me on my back, and I hauled him down with me. We kissed breathlessly, desperately, and barely missed a beat when he thrust into me. I moaned against his lips and hooked a leg around his waist, and he fucked me deep and hard.

Another moan finally forced me to break the kiss. "Oh, God, don't stop," I said, rolling my hips and dragging my nails down his back.

"You feel so good," he whispered. "But I'm not ready to come yet." He pulled out, and while my senses screamed for him to come back, my lips managed only a whimper. I desperately wanted him inside me again, but I couldn't protest the soft touch of his lips and goatee on my neck. The flick of his tongue across the hollow of my throat. The way he drew gentle, tantalizing circles around my nipple with his tongue. When he continued down my belly, kiss by gentle kiss, my back arched, and my hips squirmed beneath him. If there was one thing that could hold me over until he was inside me again, it was his mouth, and as soon as his lips were around my clit, I was halfway out of my mind.

There was no hiding what he did to me. Every sweep of his tongue made my breath catch. He held my hips down with one arm, but neither of us could keep them completely still while his tongue made those mind-bending figure-eights on my clit.

And in turn, he responded to me. Each time I gasped, his body tensed, and he shivered. When I whimpered with pleasure, he murmured against my clit and sent me even higher. The things he did with his mouth were simply incredible. He loved to talk dirty to me, and when he went down on me now, I swore he silently said filthy things to my clit.

His fingers slipped into my pussy, and it took mere seconds to find my G-spot. He stroked it, circled it, coaxing even more electricity into my senses. My breath caught, and my body shook as if I was already in the throes of a powerful orgasm, but it stayed just beyond my grasp. And still it built, intensifying with every circle of his tongue and fingertips. I was desperate for that release, but he didn't let me go, not yet. I wanted to scream for it, but I couldn't, and he kept it just out of my reach.

Just when I thought I could take no more, when I'd held my breath so long the world was turning white, he gave me the release I so desperately craved, and he didn't stop. Right through my orgasm, he kept going, striking the perfect balance of keeping me in the stratosphere without overstimulating.

From somewhere outside myself, I thought I heard my own voice begging for him to fuck me, to fuck me now, then pleading with him not to stop, not to stop, don't stop, please don't stop...

And in the instant I came the second time, he did stop, but a heartbeat later, he was over me and inside me, filling me completely and riding my breathtaking, spine-shattering climax right to the end. It went beyond the kind of orgasm that would make me scream and cry out and wake the neighbors. Like they had so many times before, his deep, eager thrusts overwhelmed me into silence, but my climax was as intense as any screaming, neighbor-waking orgasm I'd ever experienced. Like the first time I was with Austin—like *every* time with Austin—my silence was not a lack of passion, but an inability to even draw a breath,

He kissed me, his tongue sweet with the taste of me, and I wrapped my arms around him, holding him close to my trembling body and seeking every last taste of my pussy in his mouth.

Gripping my shoulders tighter, he fucked me harder, and this time the gasp, the shuddering tremor, and the moan of surrender were his. He threw his head back, and with a near-silent release of a ragged breath, he thrust all the way inside me and came.

He collapsed over me, holding me as tight as I held him, and rested his forehead on my shoulder. I ran my fingers through his sweat-dampened hair, closing my eyes and just breathing in the scent of him. The scent of us.

I can't walk away from this.

My own words echoed in my mind, and it was probably the truest statement I'd made in I didn't know how long. What I felt for him, I realized in the afterglow of such passionate lovemaking, wasn't something I could ignore, let alone abandon, no matter how challenging the circumstances.

Austin pushed himself up on shaking arms. When our eyes met, there were tears in his, and when his lips parted, I knew the words before he spoke them.

"I love you, Jocelyn."

"I love you too." And I did. For all I'd questioned this, for all I worried, I loved him. How could I not? I could barely believe there'd ever been a time when I *wasn't* in love with Austin.

Caressing my face, he said, "You said before you were worried about this happening with another client. And I know talk is cheap—it's easy for me to say it won't—but..." He trailed off, swallowing hard. "But I need you to understand something."

I put my hand over his. "What's that?"

"This hasn't happened with anyone else," he said softly. "I don't mean just clients. *Anyone.* Ever." He moistened his lips. "I've been in love before, but never like this. Not even close."

"That makes two of us." I raised my head and kissed him lightly. "I'm sorry, Austin. About what I said earlier."

"Don't be," he whispered. "This is an unusual situation. You have every right to question it."

"I know it's unusual, but I didn't…" I paused. "I wasn't setting out to call you insincere. I'm just—"

"I know, babe. I understand." He kissed me lightly. "But I think we're on the same page now."

I smiled. "Yeah, I think so."

He kissed me one more time, then pushed himself up so he could take care of the condom. When he returned, we faced each other on our sides as we often did when we talked in bed.

Austin brushed a strand of hair out of my face. "This isn't going to make things any simpler with my job."

"I don't expect it to." I combed my fingers through his hair. "We've made it this far. We'll figure it out from here. One way or another."

He nodded. "I know this is a strange situation, but I promise you, no matter what, the only thing anyone else is getting is Sabian." He kissed my forehead, then looked at me. "Austin is all yours." Then he kissed me gently and drew it out.

I knew what Austin did for a living. I knew where he was last night and the night before. I knew how and why we came into each other's lives. Lying together with him like this, though, I just didn't care, because I couldn't imagine being more in love with someone. It was hard to believe I'd even considered walking away from him, from this. What we had wasn't easy, it wasn't something outsiders could or would easily understand, but it was *right*. Whatever headache it caused, it was worth it.

He looked at me and ran his fingers through my hair.

I touched his face. "I love you, Austin."

He smiled and leaned in to kiss me again. "I love you too."

Epilogue

About a year later.

On Sunday evening, as he always did, Michael came to pick up the kids.

"Hey," he said with a smile. "Kids ready to go?"

I gestured for him to come in. "They should be. Can't promise Mikey's done with his game yet, though."

He tried to scowl. "Video games on a school night?"

"Hey, his homework is done." We started toward the living room, and I added, "That, and it's kind of hard to say no to him when someone *else* is playing."

We stopped in the doorway.

Oblivious to his parents watching, Mikey said, "I am so beating you this time."

"Not a chance," Austin said. "Because you see..." He paused. "When you spend all your time talking trash..." Another pause. Then an explosion lit up the screen, and Austin laughed. "You don't see people sneaking up on you, do you?"

"Aw, man," Mikey said. "Again?"

"Told you." Austin set his controller down. "You should pay attention instead of talking trash."

In a high-pitched, mocking voice, Mikey said, "You should pay attention instead of talking trash."

Austin threw a pillow at him. Mikey threw it back.

"All right, you two," I said. "Do I have to separate you?"

They both looked up, and damn if Austin hadn't learned to flawlessly imitate Mikey's puppy-dog eyes.

Michael laughed. "Looks like you have your hands full."

"Yeah, you could say that." To Mikey, I said, "You ready to go?"

"Let me go get my things." He set his controller down and got up.

"Where's Lex?" Michael asked.

"We went to the library yesterday," Austin said. "She's been holed up in her room with a stack of books ever since."

Michael chuckled. "That doesn't surprise me."

"Especially since someone showed her the astronomy section," I said. "She'd have taken every book off the shelf if we'd let her."

"Sounds like Lex." Michael gestured at the Xbox. "So, it looks like you're starting to beat him."

Austin rolled his eyes. "Up to level four, yeah. But I can't get near him on anything after that. Doesn't do a lot of good to win the battle if you can't win the war, you know?"

"Hey, at least you can beat him on four." Michael shook his head. "I can't touch him."

"Just wait until you get to the armory," Austin said. "Then come around the building from the left. He never sees it coming."

"I heard that," Mikey called from the other room.

Austin chuckled and winked. "Trust me. Gets him every time."

"You two," I said, rolling my eyes. "Ganging up on a kid? That's just mean."

"Mean?" Michael scoffed. "That kid has cheat codes that make him almost unbeatable. We old guys need a little help, you know?"

"All the help we can get." Austin laughed. "Oh, and speaking of which..."

While my boyfriend and ex-husband discussed the strategies and idiosyncrasies of the game and how they would one day beat Mikey, I went upstairs to make sure the kids got everything together.

The last year or so had been challenging to say the least. It was still weird, being a prostitute's girlfriend, and some nights were harder than others. There'd been a few times when I'd caught myself thinking I couldn't deal with this anymore, but we'd gotten through it. Every night he was with me, Austin made sure I knew what we had was worlds apart from the strictly business interludes with his clients. It was a job to him, nothing more, and with time, it was easier for me to accept it.

It had taken Michael a month or so and several conversations with Austin and me before he finally decided he was okay with Austin meeting the kids. Mikey had immediately taken to Austin, particularly when they found a few favorite video games in common. Mikey was also enamored of Austin's artistic talent, and the two of them spent hours at the kitchen table discussing the intricacies of composition, shading, and a few million things I didn't understand.

Alexis wasn't so quick to warm up to him. She was definitely her daddy's little girl, and after a few weeks of icy hostility toward Austin, Michael and I finally sat down with her to see what was up. Turned out she was afraid Austin was somehow trying to encroach and fill Michael's role. Once we explained he'd no more do that than Carrie had taken over my role, she relaxed.

In fact, just the other night, I'd caught Lex and Austin sitting out on the back deck, staring up at the stars and trying to convince each other of the existence of bullshit constellations. At some point, right around the time she'd been explaining to him that a certain collection of stars formed the constellation SpongeBob, his work phone had gone off.

He never took his eyes off the stars. Without missing a beat in their conversation, he casually reached into his pocket, pulled out the phone, and kicked the call over to voice mail. It didn't ring again. To my knowledge, he never returned the call, because he spent that night with his arm around me and his soft goatee against my neck.

"You guys have everything you need?" I asked from the hallway.

"Almost," Lex called from her room.

Something shuffled in Mikey's room. Then he came out with his backpack over his shoulder and a rolled-up poster in his hand. "I'm ready."

A second later, Lex appeared with a stack of books and her school bag. "Me too."

"Off we go, then," I said. The kids followed me downstairs.

When I came around the corner into the living room, Michael and Austin abruptly halted their conversation and glanced at me.

I looked at one, then the other. "What?"

They exchanged glances.

"Nothing." Austin cleared his throat. "Just video-game crap."

I raised an eyebrow, but before I could voice my skepticism, the kids brushed past me to greet their father.

"You both have your school bags?" Michael asked.

"Right here." Alexis held hers up.

"Got mine," Mikey said.

"Good Lord, child," Michael said to Lex. "You're going to break your back carrying all those books."

She held them up to her father. "You can carry them."

"Hey, now," Austin said. "The deal was you could check out as many as you could carry."

She batted her eyes. "I can, but if he doesn't want me breaking my back..."

Austin and Michael laughed. Then Austin looked at Mikey. "You've got your poster, right?"

My son held up the rolled piece of cardstock. The two of them had spent hours on that thing last night and this morning.

"When's that due?" Michael asked.

"Tomorrow," Mikey said. "It's done, Dad. Austin helped me with it."

"Can I at least see it?" Michael asked.

Mikey slid the rubber band off and unrolled the poster. It was a timeline of the American Revolution with intricately drawn pictures depicting key events. Of course Mikey had done the bulk of the work, but Austin had helped him with the layout, not to mention offering some pointers on the detail work and the wording for the labels.

"This looks great. If that doesn't get an A, I don't know what will," Michael said.

Mikey beamed, grinning at Austin.

Then Michael rolled the poster back up and put the rubber band on it. "Well, we'd better get going. You two ready?"

"Yep," they both said. The kids hugged Austin and me good-bye. Then Michael and Austin shook hands, my ex-husband and I exchanged a quick hug, and they were out the door.

Once they were gone, Austin and I went back into the kitchen.

"Ah, we have the house to ourselves for the week." I put my hands on his shoulders. "What ever will we do with it?"

"Oh, I could think of a few things." He kissed me lightly, but when our eyes met again, his expression was suddenly serious. "Before we do, though..."

My blood turned cold. "Something wrong?"

"No, of course not." He cleared his throat. "But before we do, I..." He dropped his gaze.

"Austin?"

He took a deep breath. "Listen, I've been doing some thinking."

My heart pounded, and I waited while he searched for the words.

"I've been doing some thinking, and I think you deserve better than a prostitute for a boyfriend."

White-hot panic surged through my veins. "Austin, don't—"

"Just hear me out," he said softly. "Listen, I've never been ashamed of what I do, but I'll be the first to admit it's not compatible with certain things." He paused, shifting his weight. "And I think you deserve better than a prostitute for a boyfriend, so I hoped you might consider a semi-starving artist for a husband."

My heart stopped. "Are...are you..."

One hand left my waist, and I couldn't breathe when he reached for his back pocket. He slipped his other hand into mine, and my breath caught when he went to one knee.

He held up his other hand, and the slight tremor added to the sparkle of the diamond between his thumb and forefinger. "Jocelyn..." He took a deep breath, moistened his lips, and whispered, "Will you marry me?"

I couldn't speak, but without a second's hesitation, I managed a nod. Austin slipped the ring on my finger. Then he stood and put his arms around me, kissing me gently.

"I love you," he whispered.

"I love you too," I said, struggling to keep my emotions in check.

"And I swear," he said. "I didn't use a penny that came from the escort service to pay for that ring."

I wiped my eyes and shook my head. "I don't care. As long as it's from you, I don't care." I looked up at him, swallowing hard. "What did you mean about your job? Are you..." I paused. "Are you quitting the agency?"

Austin nodded. "I've been working for the last few months to get some other income rolling. More design gigs, that kind of thing. And I may have found someone who's willing to help me sell some of my other artwork." He ran his fingers through my hair. "It's going to involve some creative budgeting on my part, but I've got enough money saved to tide me over for a while."

"Are you sure about this?" I hesitated. "I haven't made you feel like—"

"No, baby, it's nothing you've said." He touched my face and kissed me lightly. "In fact, I think that's a big part of this decision for me. I know it hasn't been easy for you, even when you've tried to pretend it was, but you've never once asked me to give it up."

"I wouldn't ask you to give up your job," I said.

"I know," he said. "But I will."

"Austin, you..."

"I want to, babe. I'll work out the finances, but if we're going to be in this for the long haul, I just can't do both at once. And I'd rather be with you for the rest of my life than try to get a few more years out of that job." He didn't give me a chance to protest—not that I would have at this point—before he kissed me again.

When he broke the kiss, I combed my fingers through his hair, my heart fluttering when the diamond on my hand caught the light.

"You know," I said, "if it'll make things smoother for you financially, you could move in here sooner than later."

He nodded. "Let's see how the kids adjust to us being engaged." He tucked a strand of hair behind my ear. "I still have a few months left on my lease anyway."

"Good idea." I grinned. "Well, can I at least talk you into staying tonight?"

Austin laughed and trailed his fingertips down the side of my neck. "Like you even need to ask."

I raised my chin to kiss him but pulled back at the last second. Eyeing him, I said, "Is this what you and Michael were talking about when I came into the living room?"

"What?" He batted his eyes. "Uh. No. It... We were talking about..."

"Video games?"

"Yeah. That."

I laughed. "You are such a horrible liar."

He grinned. "Okay, yes, that's what we were talking about." He raised his eyebrows a little. "You don't mind, do you? That he knew before you did?"

"Not in the least." I smiled. "I'm too excited to care about any of that."

"Good." He cupped my face in both hands and kissed me.

"He's not going to tell the kids, though, is he?"

"Hell, no. He promised me he'd keep it quiet." His smile turned shy. "I just needed a little preproposal encouragement, I guess."

"Encouragement? You didn't think I'd say no, did you?"

"Well, not necessarily, but..." He bit his lip, and his cheeks colored. "I was nervous, and let's just leave it at that."

"You had nothing to be nervous about," I whispered and drew him down for another kiss. That was definitely the truth. Standing with him now, his ring on my finger and my arms around him, I couldn't imagine not marrying him. I'd secretly hoped for weeks, months even, that he'd ask, and I'd still have said yes if he hadn't told me he was giving up being an escort. I was in love with him regardless of his profession.

It was hard to believe that a year or so ago, I'd been so disillusioned and frustrated with the dating world that I'd resorted to using an escort. Seven years of aggravation in the dating pool had led me up to calling Elite Escorts, and more than once afterward, I'd regretted making that call.

I had no regrets now, because now I had everything.

THE END

Lauren Gallagher

Lauren Gallagher is an erotica writer who is said to be living in Nebrask with her husband and two incredibly spoiled cats. There is some speculation she is once again on the run from the Polynesian Mafia in the mountains of Bhutan, but she's also been sighted recently in the jungles of Brazil, on a beach in Spain, and in a back alley in Detroit with some shifty-eyed toaster salesmen. Though her whereabouts are unknown, it is known that she also writes gay male erotic romance under the pseudonym L. A. Witt.

Loose Id® Titles by Lauren Gallagher

Available in digital format and print from your favorite retailer

Damaged Goods

CPSIA information can be obtained at www.ICGtesting.com
Printed in the USA
BVOW031413120213

313069BV00001B/38/P